Nabarun Bhattacharya (1948–2014) was born into a family of writers, filmmakers, artists and academics—his father was playwright Bijan Bhattacharya; his mother, writer and activist Mahasweta Devi; his maternal grandfather, well-known *Kallol*-era writer, Manish Ghatak. Educated at Ballygunge Government School, Bhattacharya went on to study geology at Asutosh College and then English literature at City College. A journalist from 1973 to 1991 at a foreign news agency, he gave up that career in order to become a full-time writer. *Herbert* was published in 1992 and won the Bankim and Sahitya Akademi awards. Some of his best-known works are *Kangal Malshat* (2003), *Ei Mrityu Upotyoka Aamaar Desh Na* (2004) and *Phyataroor Bombachak* (2004). Novelist and short-story writer, he was also a prolific poet and, from 2003 until his death, editor of the *Bhashabandhan* journal.

Bhattacharya believed that every species has a right to exist without being at the mercy of humans, and one of his landmark novels, *Lubdhak* (2006), stems from this conviction. A devoted feeder of every stray dog and cat in the neighbourhood, he was also a keen watcher of insects, reptiles and other forms of life in his garden which he tended to for at least an hour every day. He also spent a lot of his time walking through the city, exploring its streets and lanes and bylanes, soaking in the conversations and experiences of his subjects.

His funeral procession in Calcutta was a strange one indeed—ministers and prominent cultural personalities marched alongside activists, former political prisoners and a sea of have-nots, a sea of his people. An offer of a state funeral was rejected by the family—it would have gone against the very grain of what he'd stood for, and written about, all his life.

NABARUN BHATTACHARYA

Hawa Hawa

TRANSLATED BY
SUBHA PRASAD SANYAL

Seagull
BOOKS

LONDON NEW YORK CALCUTTA

Seagull Books, 2022

The stories collected in this book were originally published
in Bengali by Protikkhon in 1995 as part of the volume
Nabarun Bhattacharya, *Chhotogolpo*

Original text © Tathagatha Bhattacharya, 2022

First published in English translation by Seagull Books, 2022

English translation © Subha Prasad Sanyal, 2022

ISBN   978 0 85742 982 7

British Library Cataloguing-in-Publication Data
A catalogue record for this book is available from the British Library

Typeset by Seagull Books, Calcutta, India
Printed and bound by WordsWorth India, New Delhi, India

CONTENTS

Hawa Hawa

The orchestra fell silent; the exhausted dancing men and women retreated into the carefully constructed bower of creepers to rest, to converse softly amongst themselves. Each of their hearts was brimming over with joy; not a single face was overcast with the shade of sorrow or poverty, want or woe; as if all of them were afloat on the river of happiness.

—Dinendra Kumar Roy, *Lady Daktar-er Ledka*, or, 'The Lady Doctor's Boy'

Takes one to know one, and I know you, *Killer*-cop. A swollen head, hair shiny-slick with oil, a pair of murky eyes set in a slightly Mongoloid face, dirty Terylene bush shirt, misshapen baggy-shabby black pants, marked with white sweat-dried salt patches—I knew you the moment I laid eyes on you. Somewhere, Michael Jackson's 'Liberian Girl' is playing. Quite a feeling, a Lovetown-Lovetown feeling. My Hero Honda vision's never let me down. Knew you at once. I'm not in the killing-stabbing *line* any more. I mean, since the indiscriminate *murders* according to the state quotas has dwindled. The bosses know it too. That age is catching up. On the whole, your face and figure haven't changed all that much. And whatever has, that's changed in me as well. So, keeping an eye on a VIP residence, eh? I'm here on the same errand, boss. Right now, you and I, two charmed dungflies in the jackfruit orchard. Buzzing round the same shit.

But Killer, now a distance of many many dead bodies lies between you and I. I'm not an *amateur* revolutionary any more, I'm a full-fledged *reporter*. A press card's poking through my pocket. A pistol's poking through yours. This isn't the beginning of the seventies. It's the end of the eighties. A swirl of circumstances has *fit* us both here, in front of the hotel hosting the King of Ghazals. You're here to amp up the *security*. I'm here to see if a famous actress comes for a night ride on the Ghazal King—or not, will she come or won't she. Will she come or won't she come—she hasn't come yet. A wind is blowing. Hawa hawa.

The man who's my *editor*, he sits in an air-conditioned office, every now and then runs his fingers along his armpits and then smells them and then is filled with limitless joy; alongside, he smokes imported cigarettes. Fretting one moment and melting the next, his standing orders are to keep our eyes and ears trained on the scent, to keep our noses firmly on the trail of who is screwing whom, and how fine the screws are. Folks don't have time for words of wisdom any more. Arse wiping with the left hand and eating with the right—it's the age of the *quickie*, the fast fuck. All hail *stress* and *tension*! Look for the *masala*, hunt it down, hang it up. And the game is on! That's why when I'm here on *duty*, then a smiling spy-cop shimmies out of my memory-Babylon and stands beneath this hotel's hanging balcony, there where the carnivorous 9 p.m. air is agog-abuzz with lights and people and lice and whores. Shri Spy, it's very windy out here. Hawa hawa. Ek do teen, chaar paanch chhai—I've been counting cars all this while. Skipping the *two-wheelers*. That bitch is coming for sure. Two shops away is standing our *jeans-jacket*-wearing photographer, his name's Rat.

He's a pill popper. Looks drowsy all the time. But takes fab photos. Maruti Fiat Maruti Maruti Gypsy Ambi Maruti Spykiller—

I recognized him the moment I saw him, and I watch him now, a cigarette stylishly between my teeth, as if I'll give him a full Clint Eastwood beating as soon as I've lit up. I light up as he comes closer. Exhale up into the neon light. He bares his mottled teeth. The overwhelming sound of traffic. Glasnost, that is, openness and transparency. I'd opened. Now, it was time to be transparent.

He started the conversation.

'I *knew* I'd recognized you. I have to say, you're looking pretty OK.'

'Have we met before? I think I've seen you somewhere . . .'

'Of course you have. I followed you for two days at Digha. Remember?'

'Bits and pieces.'

'Well, it's been a while now. Do you know what it was all about? I'd have offed you then.'

'Meaning?'

'Finished you. I'd made up my mind.'

'And then?'

'Then I saw you were drunk, I mean, you were even more of a *young man* then—and completely drunk. Not a political chicken. But a *love-case* product. We get that sort of thing. Anyway, you got away by the skin of your teeth that time. So, what are you up to nowadays?'

'Reporter. I collect news.'

'Which paper?'

I told him the name. He was terribly excited. 'Your Sports page is *solid*. That *referee*-thrashing scandal—'

'Yes, many people read our paper just for the Sports page.'

'I agree. Best to stick to games and sports. Enough of politics-folitics.'

'Quite right.'

The shops are closing one by one. The curio shop closes first. A girl in cheap powder and a cascading nylon saree rubs against a pillar. Then climbs into a taxi. A happy family walk past with an enormous *vulgar jumbo* balloon. It's night, but the kids are still quite perky. We squeeze down onto the steps of the closed curio shop.

'The whores' per-night income isn't bad.'

'No, why should it be?'

'Seen the state of the market? It's on fire! The price of eggplants is making even the gourds burst out laughing. And yet, look at the skin market—no fluctuations at all.'

I guessed that his illicit-income game wasn't going too well.

'You still drink that much? The amount you drank those two days—reeking of the stuff, day and night.'

'It's not that I don't. But it's more like once in a while now.'

'That's best. Stay healthy and all else will be fine. Have a family?'

'I do.'

'Great! Just think, if that day, for joining the Naxal gang, I'd bumped you off in the bushes—I had a hot piece in my pocket, loaded too—no one's father could have stopped me.'

4

'Good thing you didn't, then.'

'Mother swear, Ma Kali swear, I'd followed you—there'd been a report—but then I saw you'd die if I killed you, you'd die if I didn't. Suicide case.'

'Who did suicide?'

'No, I mean, it's boys like you who take up with girls in college. And the kinds of girls nowadays—she rejects you, and then ghapaghap, you suicide. I've seen so many.'

'How come you know so much?'

'Brother, we're the police after all. We've seen so much so close that just a sideways glance from us is enough to X-ray you through and through. Tell me, there was a *love-case*, wasn't there?'

'There was.'

'Didn't you try to suicide?'

'I did.'

'And chickened out at the end?'

'Ekdam.'

'Happens. All suicide cases stop to think once. But do they really think? Or make others think? If the ghosts are pulling strong enough, they survive. And if not, *pop!*'

'Ghosts?'

'Arre, the ghosts of your fathers and forefathers, they're always watching you. Say, your mother's just died. That pull, that's damn strong. She'll watch over you left, right and centre. Won't let you take a single false step.'

'So you're saying they had a strong pull on me too?'

'If they didn't, would you have come back? That clangorous-clamorous sea, a *love-case*, a book of poems, a flute, a bottle of booze, a full-moon night—does anyone come back from that? It's that pull—so many different types of ghosts, not to mention souls and spirits—you think it's all nothing? There's a book I've read. It's got everything.'

'Every what?'

'Thing. Think of a good human being—I don't mean saints or sadhus, they're at an even higher level—think of someone like you or me, someone who doesn't meddle in anyone else's affairs. If one of them dies, they'll stay within a radius of around 25,000 kilometres.'

'Really?!'

'And those who've died by accident—run over by a bus, burnt, hanged, Folidol—'

'And the ones you've killed as well?'

'Yes, yes, them too—after all, those were accidents as well, right? This lot stays close to shore. And whenever they see a pothole or an empty coconut shell, that's it, they'll slip right in, and then those garbage dumps, nooks and crannies—gutters, crevices, anything like that, you'll know it's teeming with accidental deaths.'

'OK, I get the teeming part. But don't they do anything else? What about, say, the people you've killed?'

'Of course, they do. And spend all their time looking for a chance to do so. One chance, and they'll swallow you up. But they can't do anything to me.'

'Why not?'

'It's—there's a thing.'

'What? Where?'

'Let's say . . . it's right on my body. Can't show it, though. I'm telling you because it's you. I don't tell this to everyone.'

'Sounds fantastic!'

'It really is! And I'll tell you something else: say, your pull's a bit loose. Say, if your parents died long ago. Vanished up there. Not really concerned about you. How will you keep yourself safe then? How will you stay fit?'

'I guess I won't.'

'I'm telling you because you're still quite young. Don't be shy. In such a case, you've got to sex, regular bamwham. Look at me—if I nudge you right now, you'll fall flat on your face.'

'I will indeed. You've really kept your body well.'

'I've had to, brother. There're no limits to the kinds of police duty. How will I survive if I don't look after my body? Kali, Kali, it's almost Tantric practice. Whatever you eat, you'll be able to digest. Your body will tingle. Mark my words.'

'I'll mark them.'

'Tantriks, even those kapaliks—just look at their bodies! Indira Gandhi's cremation—they showed it all on TV. Did you see?

'Yes.'

'Remember Dhiren Brahmachari? The balls on him, man! It was so cold in Delhi, everyone was shivering in their overcoats. And he—totally bare chested! Holy fuck!'

The CRPF on either side of the dark Kharagpur railway platform, it seemed as if they were giving me a *guard of honour*. Even though I was wearing them, jeans hadn't come into fashion yet. I had a *kitbag* on my shoulder. Egora, Belda, Satmile—I've forgotten where exactly,

7

but after crossing some place like that, I saw in the early morning a group of khakis making their way along a dirt road through the fields, rifles slung over their shoulders. There'd been a cyclone that year. Spy-sahib had probably started on my trail from Kharagpur itself. On the bus, I'd suddenly started singing: Mor bhabonare ki haway matalo. What wind is intoxicating my thoughts?

And it was in that context that I met Mihi-dada and Danadar-boudi of Howrah. What a riotous ruckus that was! Didn't I know that the woman had been hired? Mihi-dada has a bagatelle in his armpit, aloo-dum in his lap. Hadn't that boudi treated me to a small ilish fry on the second floor of that cheap canteen? Hadn't she sung to me? And in return, hadn't I played my mouth organ for her? Hadn't this police bastard heard me play? According to this police-paid hitman's version, I was then in my high romantic *phase*. I had a book by Mario Praz with me, many others, The Collected Poems of Auden—an almost-dark restaurant where lovers eat each other up. Since I couldn't eat anything, it was time to die. Hawa hawa.

Come to me, ocean waves, spread your wings and come. Take me away. To your depths, to the deepest of your deep, where no light comes, where the transparent and eyeless shrimps swarm, their antennae waving, wondrous anemones, Foraminifera, but the seashells one can find there, they have such extraordinary colours, who knows who creates those shades, it's a puzzle we cannot solve, this is my extraordinary world, although the police spy's world is no less fantastic.

Back here, that film star, that shameless hussy, she hasn't come yet to the Ghazal King. Guess I'll have to stay pretty late. Although, of course, I'll still be able to catch a cab.

These winds, such hot winds blow through this thermocity—the killer-cop—I give him a cigarette.

'A bribe?'

'Maybe. Do you know why I'm here?'

'Why else? To poke about that slut scandal.'

'How did you know?'

'You reporters. You should all be dispatched to the Nehru Bal Museum. And the police should publish a newspaper instead.'

'You're absolutely right.'

'We're no better off—have to keep an eye on these femme fatales.'

'Why?'

'What if they get kidnapped? Didn't you hear, just a few days ago, they'd planned to abduct Rekha? Ah, such a lovely breeze . . . blowing from the Ganga.'

'Yes. You've really shaken me, by god.'

'How?'

'What you were saying again and again: "I'd have finished you." '

'I would have. If you'd stepped out of line even once. I've finished so many. But yes, only on orders. I have kids too, after all. And does anyone really like to kill?'

'Do you remember them all?'

'How can I forget? Though I think I can't do that any more. Do you know, young men, just young men—I made them stand in a row and then shot them. Makes me sick to my stomach.'

'How did it feel?'

'There's no feeling then. Just the finishing. They know they're going to get shot, their backs are against the wall and still they're shouting slogans. All the houses shut their doors and windows. Shut tight. That was in Beleghata.'

'Weren't you at the Baranagar Killing?'

'No, brother. I wasn't called for that one.'

'And?'

'Do you remember that cinema? In the south? Behind that— I took them there at night. It was their own neighbourhood. Two young men. I told them: Go, go back home quietly now. I let them go. And then, from the back—'

'They had no idea?'

'Of course they did. Everyone gets the idea. They knew full well they weren't going home. Arre these hands have begun to rot from the kills, they've killed so many. And just killing them wasn't enough. I'd kick them and see, if the heart was still beating.'

'So why didn't you finish me? Everything was *ready*.'

'Why? Like I said, you looked so forlorn. On top of that, you were clearly eyeing the girls. Murmuring something to yourself all the time. I went through your bag and found an English poetry book. A bottle of booze. And a flute.'

'Flute makes me sound a bit Krishna-Krishna. Call it a mouth organ, won't you?'

'Whatever. And then I saw you sleeping in the forest, a book under your head. The way a hen sleeps at night. I felt pity. Decided to let you go.'

If there was a camera placed nearby, it would see me suddenly leaping to my feet and breaking into a run. Rat running too, with his camera. Racing—because that film star had finally arrived! The soundtrack would be filled with my shouting.

Where do you think you're going? Room number 530. Hello, oh missus!

Rat's camera flashes. A Nikon shot of a neon beauty. Profile.

She looks at me, obviously angry. 'Oof, unbearable! What do you want?'

'*Excuse me*, do you have a special appointment with the Ghazal King? Heard you two are getting married?'

'You *swine*! He's my friend!'

'Imran Khan is your friend too, isn't he?'

'*Yes, Immy is also a friend of mine.*'

Her fans and her guard push me away. I understand the fans—but a guard? This is my unique thesis—guards are a *new class*. Been hand in hand with revolution for so long—in the middle of all this Gorbachev and Tiananmen talk, will anyone read your paper if you've not got anything new to say? Editor-sahib, your 400-rupee nylon vest, your oily sheen, your fuckery, your intelligence operations—boss, whom do you like? That voluptuous and explosive film star? Or this half-Mongoloid killer and spy?

Sorry! O Lord Killer, at once killer and spy. You're a shitty villain from a shitty film. Yes. Yes, you did smell the booze on my breath. Yes, I was lying in the forest, listening to the ocean waves, Auden's *Collected Poems* under my head and my eyes closed. 'Tis true indeed that you grew irritated, that you went back. But you went back without knowing some fantastic facts. I was carrying—to eventually hand over—a rapid-firing imported firearm, heavy, small and deadly. And loaded. Along with a letter and quite a lot of money. You didn't find anything when you went through my *kitbag* at the *cheap canteen*. And, idiot, when you were ordering omelettes at the Bay Cafe, my eyes had opened by then and I even had a few visitors. I gave them whatever I had to give. Took whatever I needed to take. And you knew nothing of this. I had my eye on you too. Instead of it being a one-sided affair, I in my turn could have sent you packing to the HMV, and not simply to record police songs. Sudden dispatch.

Assignment over. Rat's calling for a taxi. One stops.

'OK, I'm off, then.'

'Yes. It was good to see you again. When's that whore leaving, though?'

'Wait. The evening's just begun. Let her listen to a few songs first.'

'She'll listen to the songs, sit down, then you have your—'

'Tantra, yes!'

He bares his mottled teeth and smiles again.

'All right, I'm off!'

'See you!'

I climb into the taxi. Rat pretends to be asleep. I tell the driver to get going. Never again perhaps will I meet the killer and spy who'd spared my life in Digha. I'd remembered the cyclone warning, come back home quickly. That very day, the police'd killed two boys at Howrah station, dumped them on ice. They'd thought they'd killed some big leader. It was to confuse them that I'd bought along a large decorative mat, worn a necklace of seashells.

I wave, and the killer waves his killing hand at me.

Thus, a planet meets a comet. In the movies. And in life. The yellow traffic light sputters. The game of lights in this Calcutta of the night. A shiny videogame.

The song he'd sung was terrific. Hawa hawa. The hot air of the thermocity hurtles in through the taxi window.

Hawa hawa.

Mole

Close to where his *shirt* collar ends, somewhere between his shoulder and his back, he has a patch of skin about two inches wide that's infected with an itch. The skin there is soft and hairless, oily and flecked with white. The itch comes and goes depending on his desire. Just before he murders someone, the patch grows wound-wet and inflamed, itches furiously—leaks pus—then his eyes grow as cold as ice shards and he can tell that it's time to bring in another corpse. Time, full of the same desire, rubs its disfigured face against his. His desire is a living lump of flesh, covered in hair. In his right pocket, among the black cigarette crumbs, the salty sweat and the scent of sex, his pistol's black muzzle opens its eye and stares, his body feels dead and alive at the same time, his fingers are numb and yet curling mechanically, his blackish-blunt nails grow cold. The itch-worms burrow deeper into his veins, through his teeth and into his bones. The spit pools in his mouth, he sucks on his teeth, and, like an animal, scratches his back against a wall or the window grille of the police van. The rubbed-raw itch-patch starts to sting, emits a distinctively strong, sour and sweaty smell. His lips are thick and chapped. He feels like laughing then, because he understands that no one can stop the encounter now. As if the lump of flesh is telling him that, soon, he'll come back with a body—a body that's alive right now—a body that doesn't know its fate, hence any display of caution on its part remains entirely unnecessary. On his arms, the hairs ripple to attention, one by one.

The corpse is sprawled at his feet—face up or down—he pokes it with his foot. With every rattle of the van, he can tell that the corpse is settling. Sometimes it stays warm, you can smell brains, charred skin and blood. His itch fades away. He swallows his spit. Only the strong, sour odour of sweat persists. He lights a cigarette to banish the smell, his hand seeking the cigarette keeps reaching into his revolver-right pocket, the revolver feels heavy, and across his face, across his cracked-crooked teeth, writhe and wriggle the shine and shadow and gleam and glitter of the streetlamps rushing past. The van rattles on and the corpse bounces, jerks, shakes its head, as if saying no to everything, as if wanting to roll over onto the other side of darkness. The blood has dried around the charred *bullet* hole in its shirt, grown black. The eyes are slightly open or fully shut. Sometimes a gust of wind rushes in and plays with a few strands of its hair. The streetlights glint on the policemen's guns. Everyone's quiet, or speaking softly, rustic Hindi, laughing. He closes his eyes in contentment, keeps smoking. Flicks ash onto the corpse or into the darkness, prods it with his shoe. Roars out a song. The van rolls on and its rusty tin sides rattle, and the corpse, like a fool, bounces this way and that, keeping time. Just before the van drives into the police station, the black fumes of burning petrol snap him out of his reverie. By then, if the corpse has rolled over to him, if its cold hand has fallen on his foot, he kicks it away. Swears at its mother.

(When a corpse does not utter a word in response to proposals of such a nature, then a sense of authority is born in the assassin over its silent existence as well as its complete corporeality, and, after extensive training or assassinations, this tendency in the assassin, like any living thing, develops and evolves far beyond the realm of the individual. Henceforth, from the point of view of this complex consciousness, all living beings are either inanimate or deserving of death. Whether this peculiar virtue possessed by state-sanctioned assassins engages in any ghostly business with the magnetic field of bureaucracy remains a mystery, and it is possible that any attempts at investigation will prove dangerous.)

Leaning his tall, slightly hunched back against the wall, he could hear, from the other side of the dusty wooden old-case-file-storing shelf, the sound of heavy blows. Thump! Thump! A fat old lizard lives there—it hunts cockroaches, then smashes them dead against the wood. The walls, stained with swatted mosquitoes. A huge government-issue calendar. A *transistor* on Das' desk—very softly, and through an assortment of noises, the Hindi news programme plays on—but Das is asleep. He'll wake up as soon as the songs start again. The walls are so dark that, despite the two bulbs, the light is half-dead. A fly sits on the lightbulb wire. In the *lock-up*, a petty thief sings in a cracked voice. A few broken words, then the sound of *boots* on the floor. The song pauses, a lock clicks open. On his desk, an empty Coca Cola bottle—a fly buzzes in and out, his fingers itch and twitch, the radio plays on. He feels his eyes growing heavy with sleep, but he'd had a shingara that evening—his stomach is grumbling, though the good thing is that the addition of some tea to the mix will help counter the indigestion. Any minute now, the tea will arrive. The lizard (damn son of a crocodile) is still dashing dead the cockroach, though now much more slowly—the sounds from the radio mingle with the song from the petty thief—he hunches forward a little— the lizard's back is yellowish, and because it's got the cockroach in its jaws, the fucker's wings lie splayed open (the green eyes are cold . . .)—the cockroach's legs are lined with thorns, its antennae flutter feebly, the petty thief is sleepy-sprawling droop-drawling the Hindi news (two movie-ticket *blackers* sit cowering on a pile of straw in the corner—the petty thief asks for a foot massage—the constable laughs). Just as a dark dye (blood) spreads through the water, only much much more slowly are spreading . . . two headlights covered by blinkers. A tank is full of water. The water is full of bombs (for *deactivation*)—the bombs grow light in the water (Archimedes) . . . The lizard has swallowed its prey and its pale belly is swollen like a balloon . . . Blob . . . blob . . . The *silencer* kills all sound . . . Webley-Scott . . . Webley . . . fly swatter . . . That Das is fucker numero uno . . . won't even get a *posthumous* police medal . . . Picric acid, the postmortem table, nitroglycerine . . . ampoules . . . Those milk-faced *chemistry* students, bastards all of them—he sinks his hand into the water and touches the bombs . . . round objects wrapped in wet rope. Cold, yet at the touch of his hand, a hiss of white smoke . . . a flash. The cockroach-eating lizard falls on him, as do specks of sand off the wall . . . A broom scrubbing blood off the van's floor . . . OC. The curtain in his room is flying in the wind. The fan is spinning . . . Tik. BOOM . . . The explosion shakes the whole building . . . The bomb had burst in the hand of Sadhan's corpse. Its eyes had slid shut . . . its teeth so white in that burnt-black face . . . The window panes laughed themselves to bits . . . (Blue channel and its relentless message on the wireless) . . . Amid the sulphurous yellow smoke, the bombs hop and skip and jump about like balls . . .

'Have some tea, have some tea—all your sleep-sheep will go away,' Das says, holding out a glass. The eyes behind the *bifocals* are full of laughter. The moustache is laughing too. He clears his throat, picks up his glass, blows on it out of habit, then slurps a sip. Picks out a floating ant with his finger and wipes it off on the underside of the table. Das' eyes are puffy after his nap, Das is nonstop talking. 'You know, this afternoon, a *professor*—teaches in some college—dropped by. Said he wanted to meet the OC. Why the OC? But he just shook his head and said I wouldn't understand. Finally, off he went and met the OC. The rest's, of course, *evidential*—SI Mallick was in the room then, Mallick said . . . what was the word he used? Right, he said: He's writing a book about *criminal* talk. Can you imagine that? The words those thieves and robbers use! You're not understanding? Say, how they say *spy* for the Investigation Bureau, *chamber* for pistols . . . that kind of *lower-class* talk, that is. Just think, what times have come! Instead of Rabindranath and Saratchandra, they're now studying the words of pickpockets and petty thieves! What I don't understand is, why the hell have you come to the police then! You'll get to know the right words if only you spoke to the right people! Hehehe, just think—works at a college and teaches criminal talk. I can't imagine it. Hehehe—' Das talks on and on, laughs on and on. Das is quite the gossip. He's a good guy. Not a gameplayer, yet he's not entirely convinced about him. His instinct is that Das is afraid of him. Even when he smiles, his eyes seem bitten with fear. He drinks his tea with a sense of great contentment and continues to listen to Das. Smiles a little. Excited voices. He swirls the glass to dissolve the sugar. The sound of *boots* distracts him. No doubt the story is funny, but before he can say anything, SI Mallick comes running in. Trips on the door frame in his rush. He's young, restless with excitement. He lowers his voice and says, 'Gautam Biswas is at the Kalitala Youth Club's function. Listening to music. Our man Koton's informed us just now. *Authentic report.*'

Mallick is panting. The veins on his forehead are throbbing. *Nervous type.* He leaps to his feet long before Mallick has finished. The hunched back is straight now. He bottoms up the tea, smacks the glass back on the table and then, tightening his belt, strides out of the room.

Das says, 'Mallick-babu, what did you say?' But they're gone already. Das stares at them leaving, then places his ear against the radio. Along the side of the left-behind tea glass trickles down a stream of sugar . . . down and down. He turns up the radio. A van *starts* up outside. A scream. The constable's *boots* run along the veranda. This is Akash Vaani's pentachromatic presentation.

Gautam Biswas—even though he doesn't indulge in *action*, he's a deep-level *organizer*. Son of a bitch has been missing for a long time. *Authentic report. Authentic* . . . The fellow will have to be very clever in the middle of that crowd. If he runs, the shit hits the fan. Walking along the veranda, he asks Mallick, 'Is it a big crowd?'

'Yes. They've got a *Bombay artiste*.'

A big crowd for a *Bombay artiste* . . . Mallick's still quite raw . . . one glimpse of blood and he'll upend his guts . . . somewhere in that crowd stands Gautam Biswas, listening to the music . . . a long time on the run . . . just like that cell *secretary* of the Medical College . . . a sly bastard . . . finally the fucker's case file will be closed . . . the window glass is mottled, covered in mesh. When the headlights blaze on, their long beams light up the police-station gates.

He sits beside the van driver, Gurung. Four plainclothes leap aboard. The weight of their bodies causes the springs to screech and the van to swing from side to side. Then it sets off, and they pull the rear doors shut. Round holes cut into the window mesh. The van passes through the gates and jolts its way round the corner. The headlights shine on a stray dog running away.

His back is itching now. His eyes have narrowed, grown small and cold. His mouth is filling with spit. Spit flecked with bits of tobacco. He moves his fingers—they are slightly numb, and cold. He reaches into his pocket and pulls out his revolver, screws on the silencer. His fingerprints are on the barrel. If he runs through that crowd, he won't be able to shoot. Of course, if he gets to run at all. The light from the street lamp reaches through his slightly parted lips and flickers against his teeth. Quiet!! Someone in a white shirt comes up behind them on a cycle. Gautam Biswas' face comes to mind. If not the real one, at least the *photograph* one. His mouth is filling with spit. Gautam Biswas. He can see the *photograph* clearly. The van takes another turn. It's moving very fast. Sparks fly in the almost-pitch-black street. He puts a lot of oil in his hair, the wind cannot ruffle the heavy strands. The van brakes suddenly, a screech. The *headlights* shine on the wall of a girls' school. A poster. A Bombay *artiste's* come, so there's a big crowd. The van slows down, turns off its *headlights* before driving on. He's listening to the music. He tells Gurung to stop opposite the Kali temple. The van inches forward. The Youth Club's field is just a few houses away. They pass a *library* building, its brickwork visible. Gurung is an excellent driver. During the Second World War, he drove a *truck* for the *army* in Arakan. An expert hand. Almost without a sound, the van comes to a stop in the dark.

He opens the door and gets out. His gaze flickers this way and that. A few people are loitering, they look at him, his itch snarls in rage and stings. He walks on, grimaces and scratches it once. Two plainclothes walk behind him, about twenty armlengths back. They're wearing dhotis, *boots* and baggy terylene shirts. Pistols, tucked at their waists. They're trying to tread as softly as possible, but he can hear their boots. His body is straight . . . taut . . . His posture, like a snake about to strike. His left arm hangs limp. His right hand is in his pocket. Lights, people. Lots of people. Loudspeakers. Clutch . . . Like a button on a torch, the safety catch glides forward.

The mercury lamps and tube lights have turned night into day. The place is teeming with people. A short bald man finishes his *comic* sketch—a father bemoaning his son fooling around with the neighbour's daughter. The audience has laughed so hard they've broken into a sweat, the boy'd been hopping about threatening to peto-bomb his belly, of the girl's father, that is. The boys were winking at the   shy girls at the same time as they were watching each other with ferocious eyes, every man trying to maintain his own lead. A mechanical kee . . . ee . . . ee is issuing from the loudspeaker. Then it stops and an announcement blares forth: 'Now, before you, will be singing Sri Ajit Kapoor and Co.! Accompanying him on the bongos is Master Limbo, on the piano accordion is Ganesh Modak and on the guitar is Pinaki Bose!' The air grows thick with whistling. People crane their necks to get a glimpse of the stage. The musicians arrange their instruments. The mike-walla tinkers with the *microphone*. Then the announcer screams dramatically: 'Ajit Kapoor and party!' The function occupies a large open area, surrounded by a bamboo fence. Covered by a shamiana. Crowds have gathered on either side of the fence. Ajit Kapoor reaches out a hand to grasp the mike . . . the crowd stops buzzing . . . suddenly, a boy climbs on top of the fence and yells 'Hare Krishna Hare Ram!'—his face is covered with acne—a few more whistles—screams of 'Guru! Guru!' The boy's shouted request perhaps doesn't reach the singer's ears. He gives a shake to his shoulder-length hair and says, 'Our first song is from the movie *Ankh Micholi!*' More whistles. More cheers. (He was making his way through the crowd then, and when he bumped into a rather harmless-looking man, that man whispered through his teeth, 'In front of the stage, to the right . . . ') The piano accordion plays, the guitar starts to vamp, the bongo beats, tig-dig-tig-dig. The red-guru-shirt wearing singer-star leans back a little and then suddenly throws his head forward, and the young boys, weak-kneed with anticipation, watch entranced as he, at the third vamp, lifts a hand to cover an ear—as long as your eyes were shut, who had balls enough to say he wasn't Kishore Kumar?

> ' . . . aaja re aja—chhup-chhupke pyaar hum karenge
> Baat yeh kisi ko maloom ho naa paaye
> Aaja re aaja . . . '

> 'Come, baby, come—we'll make hush-hush love
> No one should get to know about us
> Come, baby, come . . . '

(The itch is tearing him apart, the lights are dissolving, through the whistles and the crowd he edges forward, his eyes search every face, he pushes people out of the way and moves on, stands on tiptoe for a better look, the front seats are full of girls, and though the right side is a little far away, but that's where . . . 'In front of the stage, to the right.')

The boy who'd yelled out the name of the film, he's cleared a bit of space amid the crowd and is dancing in the circle with his chums. Using his handkerchief as a veil, uncovering and covering his face. The others clap loudly, keeping time with his dancing-girl moves, the desire for sex more than obvious in the jerk and thrust of their hips.

> 'Kitna accha hai yeh mauka,
> Duniya bhi ho jaye dhoka,
> Jungle mein mangal manayenge hum.
> Mohabbat ki kismat jagayenge hum.'

'The chance is just right,
The world can't see this sight,
We'll make merry in the jungle
Awaken our love with a rumble-tumble.'

The girls watch, overwhelmed and awed, because some songs can bewitch the hormones, can bring a body to the threshold of opium intoxication, whether that body be young or not. The fingers of the piano–accordion player skitter across the reeds; the bongo player's hair falls across his forehead, he shakes it off. The song holds the crowd tight, the crowd is spellbound. (Gautam Biswas is the one in the blue shirt and pyjamas. Fair. Can't tell if he's paying attention to the song or if his mind is elsewhere.) He moves forward, stands a little distance away, one man away. Automatically, his right hand slips out of his pocket, holding the pistol . . . holding it with the muzzle lowered to the ground . . . what if someone saw . . . the boy's fair . . . rough hair . . . his face wears an amused expression . . . his eyes are very beautiful . . . SOS. Just one man away . . . those buggers are still dancing, he can hear their claps.

The itch leaps and lunges, his jaws grow slack . . . the spit whirlpools in his mouth. His eyes are cold, his eyes are like a dead vulture . . . his black-nailed finger coils around the trigger . . . snake . . . a moment as excruciating as when his tongue grazes against his broken teeth and slits open and starts to bleed . . .

'Aaja re aaja . . . '

He stands straight. Ready to strike. All the lightbulbs suddenly explode. In the liquid light, he pulls away the negative-image man and steps forward. Yanks a fat man out of the way and takes another step. The spit trickles through a crack in his fat lips—the bulbs have melted, the light drips in drops, drop after drop. He sticks the gun almost into the boy's belly and pulls the trigger. Blob. The boy's widening eyes. The sound stifled by the silencer. Blood spurting. The boy opens his mouth and tries to swallow air, tries to walk but his knees buckle. The sudden attack has robbed his eyes of speech, they are mute . . . spit dribbles down his chin. The boy seems to be reaching out to him, trying to touch him. But he can't, his knees cannot hold and the body falls . . .

He takes a step forward, then just beneath the skull, right against the throat, he places the mouth of the gun—and shoots. Blob. The body hurls away . . . the disgusting sound of sucking spit . . . his hands tremble briefly . . . everyone is screaming . . . the faint odour of cordite and blood . . . the lights swing to and fro . . . everyone begins to run . . . to scream . . . all the lights have fused into one flaming ball . . . then they bubble and boil and split . . . sounds . . . the sound of the lizard smashing its cockroach prey . . . blood everywhere . . . blood on people's feet . . . he rubs his face—stretches his arm . . . stops. A bloody corpse lies huddled at his feet.

Blood has splattered on an old man's shoes, the old man's pissed himself. A girl's had a fit and fainted. Some women and children are crying. The two plainclothes can't get through the crowd. A few men (policemen) are screaming: 'Don't run! Stop, don't run!' The sound of a silencer (weapon for stealthy kills) hadn't travelled far but news of the kill has—to everyone. A few terrified Youth Club boys are dashing about, trying to stop the audience from fleeing. The singer and his band are still on stage, too stunned and afraid to move. 'Don't run, don't run—stand wherever you are—nothing to worry!' One policeman heads towards a cluster of the function's organizers (that man who'd told him where Gautam was). They were saying that, after such a catastrophe, it was only right that the function be stopped, after all Gautam was a boy from as close as the next neighbourhood, besides the sight of all that blood and gore was making everyone nauseous. The policeman shouts, almost an *order*: 'Tell them to start. You're not to stop this function-tunction. Let him sing. Come on, start singing. Carry on singing. We'll take the corpse away. Start, start!' Waving his pistol at the stage like an orchestral conductor, he shouts: 'Make the announcement!'

The loudspeakers announce: 'Our musical programme is resuming. Please take your seats, and please be patient. Don't be afraid. There's no reason to be afraid.' The voice coming through the loudspeaker quivers. The man who is speaking is having trouble with his words.

The grave air of death has touched every soul. Some still have their hands up ('Don't be afraid, there's no reason to be afraid'). He starts to walk, still holding his pistol. The crowd parts to let him through, stares at him with fearful eyes. Two plainclothes follow, carrying the corpse. One holds onto an arm, the other a leg, the body hangs between them—the head helplessly dangling from the bloodied neck. Eyes wide open. The head nods along, keeps time with their steps, as if granting wholehearted approval to this much-observed journey. Blood stains his shirt. His mouth hangs open, his face still looks shocked. He'd fallen forward, so his forehead is grazed, his face is streaked with dirt. The blood trickles down his neck and past his ear and pools in his hair, drips to the ground ('Don't be afraid, there's no reason to be afraid'). His right leg scrapes along the dirt as they carry him, his fingers too, as if they want to scratch marks into the earth. Behind the corpse, that same man with a pistol. The loudspeaker crackles mechanically once more, but a few notes from the piano accordion drown it out. There, where the boy fell, the pool of blood starts to thicken. Drops of blood. Drops sprayed, drops splattered. One single sandal, lying upside down. Someone says they should sprinkle powdered lime. It's a good absorbent. ('Don't be afraid, don't be afraid. There's no reason to be afraid.)

(Sometimes they stood it up, stuck the gun behind its skull and shattered it with a bullet so that the brains splattered out, sometimes they coated it with acid and salt and buried it in the ground, set it on fire, threw it from a moving car so that no nocturnal jackal went hungry—in this context, it's important to mention that it cannot be stated with any certainty that Calcutta's canines have never tasted human flesh—hurled it into the water—when it putrefied and swelled up like a rubber ball, it would be impossible to identify— dropped it from various heights, beat it to pulp, used many other local and imported techniques . . . chemistry . . . disfigurement. Among the few things that had proved impossible, mention may be made of the Nazi *freezing mixture* and their *gas chambers*, and the American technique of throwing it off a helicopter.)

Don't be afraid. There's no reason to be afraid.

The enormous van had driven up. Its doors are flung open. He stands to one side and orders the corpse to be put in. The one holding onto its hand pulls it a bit higher, jumps in. The head bumps on the foot step. The legs hang outside. Someone pulls it in deeper, and it disappears into the darkness. One foot is missing a sandal.

Murder! Corpse-theft! Drops of blood all along the way . . . Blood from a body . . . But this blood won't be sniffed by the police dogs, their noses wrinkling as they try and track the scent of the killer . . . Aaja re aaja. Chhup-chhupke . . . How it wrenches the heart, boss! A careless postmortem . . . Yuck . . . The daily festival at

Katapukur morgue. Vans ferrying corpses to the crematorium in the dead of night. The sleepy but used-to-it dom. The naked angel flung into the glowing red coils of the *electric* furnace. The hair and clothes crackling aflame. Everyone knew it, everyone had been witness. But this time, why won't anyone witness this time? Had anyone heard a ghost talk? Gautam will show his face at the police station and then go off to the morgue. Stay there alone, all night. His mouth hanging open a little. His eyes wide open in shock. Cold ... hard ... stiff. It'll be night by the time the news gets home. Gautam's old father will startle awake at the brisk knocking on the door, grope near his pillow for his glasses.

'Who's there?'

'Open the door. Who's Haren Biswas?'

The torch will shine on the old man's frightened face. Fear will shatter the night. The sound of boots. He'll be told: come with us, it's urgent. Everyone will try to ignore the stifling suspense. So many things can happen, but anything other than death seems impossible now. Will they hand over the body? The only consolation: Gautam will know nothing of this, nothing at all. He'll spend the night, alone, in a dimly lit morgue, cold ... hard ... stiff ... memorial plaque, gallows, Golgotha. The blood has thickened into a pool. Drops of dried blood line the path they took on their way back from the hunt, carrying their prey. The air is wet with blood. No judicial investigation committee will conduct a kangaroo court for this death. Gautam cannot hope for more respect than a rape case or a wagon breaker. Blood will dry back into dust. The scent of blood will turn to breath and live inside the hearts of men. Blood. Murder. Blood. Corpse. Blood, but this time the hounds from Lal Bazaar won't sniff along on its trail. Why not?

The two *headlights* glow like Gestapo eyes. The van's moving fast, but the air of urgency is gone. He was prodding the corpse with his foot every now and then, and smoking, his eyes closed. Now that the itch is gone, he feels a bit drained. His head feels light. The van rattles, the corpse jerks and bounces. (In the early seventies, did Gautam's mother become a *paralytic* because he refused to take pride in his emasculated existence? Because of an accident? A *protein* deficiency? Gautam—'No choice but to fire two rounds in self-defence.' Lakhs and lakhs will read this news tomorrow—what can you do about it? Can you stop this giant rotary machine? Freedom of the press? You're shaking your head so much from side to side that I can't quite tell what you think.) One leg is folded under. He flicks some ash on the corpse and softly hums a tune. The cigarette smoke hits his brain. The lights crawl all over his face. A private bus wasn't giving them way. 'You motherf—' the driver swears at it. He laughs. In his pocket, the black cigarette crumbs, the trapped beads of sweat, the scent of sex and the weight of the pistol. The itch is almost gone. Has the strong, sour smell of sweat grown faint or has the smell of blood grown stronger? The light from the street lamps quivers across his oily forehead, his coarse cheek. Cast in a Fascist mould, a common and illiterate face. He feels drowsy, prods the body with his foot. Still flesh. An hour or two later, it'll be as stiff as a board. 'Stick to the floor, fucker, stick to the floor.' (No drums play on the night when they take Durga to the river. Everyone tries to forget her. No boys beat the drums and dance. Nor spray petrol from their mouths and light the air on fire. What celebration is this? Gautam, how are the morgue rats so healthy and muscular? Gautam! When they cut you up, what will they be seeking? For what have you been offered as sacrifice? Aren't you afraid?) Black burnt-petrol fumes waft into his nostrils. The van lurches. He can't hold the cigarette to his lips. The corpse bounces uncontrollably. The van goes through the gates of the police station. The rumbling engine finally falls silent. The headlights grow dark.

Another black van, a white cross on its side. Two khaki-clad, frail, semi-old men. They'll take Gautam to the morgue in that van. Even though it was called an ambulance van, it tended to transport more of the dead than it did the living. The smell of iodoform . . . dissection . . . mice scurrying about. Gautam, won't you be afraid?

He was loosening his belt as he walked in. To the OC's office, to report.

'Did he put up any resistance?'

'No, sir, didn't have time.'

As he is leaving, the OC asks, 'How many rounds?'

'Two rounds, sir.' (Could've done it with one, but it's hard to stop these fingers when murder possesses them.)

Walking back into his room, he hears Rabindrasangeet playing on Das' radio. The room is empty. Das comes in a little later. Sounds of laughter float in from the women's lock-up. He pricks up his ears. Das starts to talk, talks on and on. 'Just see, what nonsense they're up to. Arrested a bunch of floozies. You went out on *duty*. And these idiots walked in with them. If you're going to arrest girls and bring them, go ahead. But why bring them to me? What a mouth each one has! Wholly wholesale! They talk and they laugh . . . they talk and they laugh . . . Really, shame-shame!'

SI Mallick enters. Das says 'Oh sir! That professor or parasol who came this afternoon—what was that thing he kept saying all the time?'

Mallick doesn't understand. 'What thing?'

'Come on! All that street talk of crooks and thieves! Spies, bishops, all that!'

Mallick smiles a little and says, 'Slang. He's writing an *underworld-slang* dictionary.'

'That's it that's it, sleng! Got it. He collects sleng. Sleng!' Das bursts into laughter, his head shaking from side to side. The girls in lock-up also burst into peals of laughter. They're laughing so hard, they're almost falling over each other. He listens closely. It's quite enjoyable, the sound, he likes it. The scent of powder and tobacco leaves . . . broad-broad, black-black. Thick-thick lips and a broad nylon *ribbon* in the hair. 'Fuck! I've been beating these fuckwits for so long, my hand is rotting away!' He gets up and goes to the toilet.

(Immediately upon sensing that one has acquired the right to destroy another, a feeling akin to the desire to kill but in the guise of a fear of death is born, in the blood cells, in the consciousness, in the nerves, and it both excessively arouses and renders weak this new generation's anarchic body at the same time as it makes the mind more cautious and susceptible to prejudice. Within this contradictory destructive current, negativity increases exponentially and renders tired and dull the instinct for self-preservation, as a result of which every killing catalyses within one one's own death, as a result of which in his blood there echoes the buzzing of a hundred thousand plague flies' wings, fluttering triumphantly.)

He was on the seat near the door, his head drooping, swinging from side to side. On his way back at night, the shaking of the relief van was lulling him to sleep. But that old habit of searching for something near his feet, that banishes the drowsiness again and again.

Back home, he usually takes a bath, uses soap—puts some ointment on the itch—the sweat from his body and the dirty soap-lather swirl into the drain and disappear. He rubs scented oil in his hair. He is very sleepy, but sleep never comes without dreams. Dreams have eyes, they ask questions, they laugh, they beat on drums. Their limbs are ripped and shredded, bits and pieces, bloody. His family has told him he sometimes talks in his sleep, groans, slurs out orders. Sometimes he scratches his back so furiously that he wakes up in the morning to find it bleeding. Earlier he thought it must have been ghosts at work. Then the patch would itch through the day, and his right hand would grow restless. The man beside him is drowsing too. Someone's smoking a bidi—its tip glows for an instant. Sleep makes his head hang loose and low . . . his ear is full of the van's hum as it drives on . . . his left leg slides forward. The only light is from the streetlamps. Most of the houses are dark. A few people in front of a paan shop. The tram workers have dug up the tramline, they're working. Red lamps sit perched on mounds of dark dug-up earth. But he's dozing, so he doesn't see any of it. The dark cinema hall—an enormous poster of a heroine—the lips clawed away. The streets are empty—the last few taxis billow puffs of smoke and scatter. Duty over, a private bus is going back to its garage, its lights turned off. He dozes, his tiffin box clutched in his left hand, but an acute sixth sense seems to let him know exactly which street they're on, which crossing. If he opens his eyes, he'll see familiar places.

His own neighbourhood is quiet. The van drops him off at the mouth of the lane, picks him up from there every morning. His neighbourhood doesn't get into trouble. There's some graffiti on the walls, but that's the work of boys from elsewhere. He knows very well that no boy from here would do such a thing. Every night, as he comes back home, he thinks deeply about such things. Weighs every word, dwells on it, yet his fear persists. There is no way in which he can be completely reassured, because Sudhir Bose had been an SI at the same police station too. His neighbourhood too had been a quiet one, but right at his doorstep someone hacked him to pieces. His right hand rubs against his pocket, touches the pistol. Of course, Sudhir'd had some disadvantages—he'd a tendency to run to fat, so he wasn't too quick with his hands and feet. Every chance he got, he'd stand in front of the mirror and primp the parting in his hair. Rumour had it that he'd still run about twenty armlengths, clutching his hacked-open belly. Had a wife, two kids. He'd been there that day, when van after van formed a procession to the crematorium, carrying Sudhir's body. He'd looked very closely: his face was all right but his belly had been slashed wide. He hadn't died on the spot either: clung to life for a day or two, a tube running up his nose. Before the van comes to a halt, he puts away the tiffin box in his left pocket. Takes the pistol out of his right—quite heavy—checks the magazine— takes off the safety, puts his finger round the trigger and puts his hand back in his pocket. The van stops.

The engine's still running, a groaning sound. He opens the door, jumps out. Shuts the door. The van drives off. The small, red light and the mechanical groan both disappear into the distance. No one, empty. Only the sickly pale light of the moon. No light shines in any of the houses. The van's groan can be heard no more, silence thickens around him. A cool breeze. He turns the corner, the lane's quite narrow, the van can't get in. The boundary wall on the left seems to be rolling backwards as he walks. The broken bits of glass set on top of the wall sparkle in the moonlight. Only the sound of his footsteps. A little away from the moon, a cloud. A little more away, a lamp post. Suddenly he stops. His footsteps fall silent. His hand slips out of his pocket, holding the pistol. Something is scraping its way towards him, coming closer, as if to touch.

The streetlamp rolls to the ground in a burst of laughter. On the other side, the gaunt wall bares its brick teeth at him and laughs. An eye inside a crack, the eyelids torn off . . . the yawning maw of the *hydrant* and someone with an ear against it, listening. One knife of revenge screams through the air, and misses. The blade like a flame. From the back, like a bullet spat out of the barrel of a homemade gun, a sharp light rushes at him. Clutching his pistol, he looks around, his eyes flicking about like a snake's. Walls, blackened moss, silent night. Yet the yellow moon is falling off the rooftops and onto the road and shattering into countless splinters. In his body, in his flesh and blood, in his bones and marrow, in his veins, is gathered fear—fear! The fear of death, like a silent executioner, stands frozen in that terrifying darkness, so dark as if all the stars have fallen to their deaths. The ground trembles beneath the hooves of an infinite cavalry seeking revenge. The sound of bare feet running . . . *Stab case* . . . Halal. Blue shirt, white pyjamas, a handkerchief round his mouth . . . the remarkable aim of a man holding his shawl around him with one hand and hurling a bomb with the other . . . 'Victory will be ours!' The sound of revenge in the damp air of the morgue . . . In the crematorium, at the horizon . . . The sound of revenge roams the streets, swallows home after home . . . the boy's bloodless face . . . *dagger* . . . bloodied-blue shirt . . . The bullet holes in his body glow and fade, glow and fade . . .

He's panting, snorting. Fear makes his body crumple— his breath, *blood group*, spit, ID card, thumbprint, smile, revolver, *passport-size* photo, low IQ, digestion, happiness, prostitute, consciousness, country, zodiac sign—like napalm jelly, rendered clear, dense, terrible—his existence shrivels like a frightened roundworm.

That scraping sound. He looks around—no one. That scraping sound. An old election poster hangs loose, flaps against the wall. That scraping sound.

His body grows taut again, his face almost slothful and contented. He takes the pistol in his left hand because his right palm is slippery with sweat. Wipes it dry on his pants. The excitement causes the spit to trickle down his chin. He wipes his face and smells that strong, sour odour of sweat. The organic smell of death and fear. The sound of his footsteps grows louder. He glances at the moon and sees it still stuck to the rooftop. Parting his lips, his teeth emerge yellow— he smiles. A cat runs across the street, disappears into a fishy-smelling mound of ash and rubbish. He smiles. His eyes are alert, glowing. His shadow is split between the street and the boundary wall—the gutter runs through his chest. A crooked metal sign bears the *Corporation* notice: 'Urinate Here'. 'Don't' has been scratched off with a brick. A vomit-making stink. A few insects fluttering around the street lamp—they cannot hear the sound of his footsteps. The houses in the dark, like vast animals waiting for their prey. Fear prompts his teeth to stop smiling and hide behind his lips again. Spit pools in his mouth. The moonlight dazzles. His fingers curl in annoyance. The sour desire crawls down his fingers and collects in his blackish, blunt nails.

Close to where his *shirt* collar ends, somewhere between his shoulder and his back, does that patch of skin start to itch?

Long Live the Counter-Revolution

I returned from Mercury to Calcutta, yesterday. This is the last time I'll experience a return to Calcutta. After this, I won't come back any more. I'll stay on in Mercury. I've got a *cell* there. Where the sky comes down and hits your back as soon you stand up straight. Or I could go to another city. But this is my last train ride back to Calcutta. And because I don't leave anyone behind, I feel so bad as, all alone, I touch every platform of the night along the way. In the beginning, I mean, when the green light pushes the train on its way, I feel I'll never be hungry, never fall asleep. But just a little later I am in fact hungry. Sitting by the open window, I find it hard to be travelling alone. But with an impossibly grave face, I keep on eating. Then at some point I even fall asleep. The train carries me on, towards Calcutta.

The train runs along; darkness tries to run away on either side of the tracks but trips over the signal wires and falls flat on its face. The wind howls and clutches the trees to its chest. The sleepy land of coolies, shunters, *brakemen* and *firemen* afloat in the glow of yellow lamps. Red, red, red light signals. The sky, the fields, the rail lines criss-crossing the enormous yards, the sound of rocks exploding in a faraway mountain mine, the sound of switching tracks that hammer at your heart, a cargo train suddenly appearing by your side and the grass-covered buffer at the end of an abandoned railtrack—

A cool breeze blows over my feet, and there's a damp towel crumpled under my head.

I see clearly in my sleep that, after the Green Revolution, there's not even one farmer left on Mercury. Everyone's in the morgue. Yet the fields and the farms are flooded with wheat. The few farmers that're still free, they have no room to stand. Where will they stand if there's wheatgrass everywhere? Instead of wasting this surplus wheat, they send it to America. Of course. People in America are starving yet Mercury is overflowing with wheat. The train carries me on, towards Calcutta. I'll tell you later how I'll get there. My return is in one way a good thing. Because, in-between, for quite a few days, I hadn't been good to myself. At least, that's what I'll believe if someone tells me so. Didn't write a single letter, didn't think even once about how I was. That's why, as soon as we met, I had that 'tell you everything later' air. I did tell everything later. After listening to everything, he simply put his hand on mine. That meant that every-thing was all right now.

Everything was all right now, though it was not possible that it should be so. Because when we'd been called from home, we'd walked together to the edge of the small bridge. There where the crabs have dug holes and it's muddy, there another person and I had winked at each other. Then that person had shoved him in the chest. He'd fallen face-down in the mud. Tried to get up. My first shot hit him in the waist. Crumpling up, he tried to push himself through the mud with his elbows, scrape his way out. The broken bits of snail shells scratched a tear at his throat. The next shot I fired after I went down to the mud, held the gun to his head. Then that other person and I dragged him to the water. When we were in waist deep, his body rolled over. I put the revolver back in my pocket, washed my hands. When I stood up again, I saw his body stuck against one of the columns of the bridge. His face now turned towards us. The other one picked up a couple of bricks, got to the top of the bridge and dropped them on him. Their weight dislodged him, pushed him away. Then he slowly floated off, diagonally, on the waves. After all this, I at least had thought that we could arrive at an agreement. And that is what happened in the end. Now he and I are the same. The cold wind has made my toes stiff. Moonlight falls on my nails.

This was the diary they found when they searched my room—

5–3–73 (Midnight)

It is quite probably all over. I still believe in my every word. Before this, I have been shattered each time—naturally, as waves of disbelief entangled with the desire of suicide that tormented and intoxicated me. My previous acts are almost comparable to Black September— a bit of hate, a bit of indignation—mindless and ferocious like an avalanche, or a sinking ship. Surprisingly, I'm much more composed now. The silence of he who has turned mute after losing all faith in words. Like the *asphalt*, the air or water, I am without form. Like the *lamp post*, I am pensive and alone. In one grown so old, sorrow has no choice but to assume a different shape. My calm, Buddhist mind, self-contained within its own rules, is unfamiliar to me. It may even be that I'm dead, that someone else is thinking. If suicide could really be the death of two together, I wouldn't hesitate. I'm not me any more—I am someone else. If he stays for long enough, maybe I will learn to know them.

'Communists, Red sympathizers and their families are being massacred by the thousands. Backlands army *units* are reported to have executed thousands of Communists after *interrogation* in remote rural jails. [. . .] Armed with wide-bladed knives called parangs,

Moslem bands crept at night into the homes of Communists, killing entire families and burying the bodies in shallow graves. [. . .] The murder campaign became so brazen in parts of rural East Java that Moslem bands placed the heads of victims on poles and paraded them through villages. The killings have been on such a scale that the disposal of the corpses has created a serious sanitation problem in East Java and northern Sumatra, where the humid air bears the reek of decaying flesh. Travelers from those areas tell of small rivers and streams that have been literally clogged with bodies; river transportation has at places been impeded.*

Dark-eyed dogs remind me of you. The sound of trains reminds me of you—like now. The songs of Negroes remind me of you. Every time, every thing brings you to me and when nothing could be seen through the darkness then by the light of your body I bent to touch you in a tender and restless darkness I can hide you but I haven't become quite natural yet although I am rather unnatural you've kissed my eyes and I've peered between your lips.

On the evening of your arrest, if you keep looking at the 500- or 1000-watt-bright round white lights, you can't see who's behind them. They asked questions. But I refused to answer. After four hours, they turned off the lights and fed me. Gave me a place to sleep. And then as soon as the first sleep came, they yanked me out and put me back before the lights. The lights turn off again and again, but the heat from them remains. I feel as though my brains are on fire. The interrogation carries on for another four hours, but I can't see the one who's asking the questions. The smell of the leather *holster*, and

---

Time, 'Indonesia: Silent Settlement', 17 December 1965 (available at: https://bityl.co/EotD; last accessed on 27 September 2022).

through the dark, along with the questions, the spit and the breath from a stinking mouth come rushing at me.

You taught me how to kiss and when I got a little tired of kissing you I smelt the beautiful fragrance of your mouth and our eyelashes touched but because we couldn't stay like that for long I sat on the edge of the bed and groped about the desk for cigarettes and because the flaming matchstick would light up the place I hid the flame with my hand but I knew that in that flash of reddish light you saw my face and my dishevelled hair I dropped the match on the floor and looked at you and as soon as the cigarette was lit by that light I saw your face you're staring you take my hand and put it on your breast and cover mine with yours and say to me that my fingers are impossibly beautiful.

The first spike of pain when the needle is forced under your fingernails feels like your nerves are tearing and rapidly recoiling into your shoulders. The person pushing the needle is leaning forward in his chair, making disgusting noises with his mouth. The fan is spinning. My hands are *strapped*. The needle goes under my nails to the very end. The blood around the needle screams in fear. The needle touches bone and tries to push through, then stops. Then when I look at my hand, I see swollen such veins and arteries of whose existence I was, until then, entirely unaware.

I've never seen anyone like you. No one can love me so unconditionally no one's love can be so complete so unquestionable no eyes hold so much agreement no blood has been born with so much support running through it.

The Nazis killed a 120,000 Jewish infants. The first Nuremberg trials revealed that they murdered even the cognitively disabled children.

I love you see how the train rushes through the dark field now I love you on the night train I'd stood at the door and seen far away some people gathering dry leaves under a tree and lighting a fire in the darkness the sound of your breath as if you've fallen asleep so I stand up to leave and try not to wake you but you tell me in your sleepy voice about the night's last kiss and I'm here for a taste of you again.

The sick babies were killed by *machine guns*, were starved to death or thrown out of the windows. In Upper Silesia's Lubliniec hospital, Luminal and Veronal (0.1 to 0.6 gram) were used on 235 children, aged between 8 months and 10 years. Of them, 221 died. And in Eglfing-Haar, near Munich, Dr Hermann Pfannmüller used to kill the children with his own hands. Because all the other methods proved too costly, he took to starving them to death.

I love you believe me I love you I place my hand upon you and swear it.

According to the German government's *report*, in 47 days sometime between 1944 and '45, 99,922 pairs of children's shirts and underwear were dispatched to Germany from the Auschwitz-Oświęcim death camp.

Switch off the darkness for I love you switch off the darkness now for I love you.

... This is the diary they found when they searched my room ...

5–3–73 (After midnight)

[Continued from the last entry]

I am not angry in the least, I feel both scattered and level headed. It is probably this second or third self that will not let me do anything unnatural. Because its intellect is much greater, its tolerance is greater too. If I stay smiling and still like this for some time, then maybe I'll know that I've arrived at my full potential—this is the one I've been searching for in all my restlessness. You cannot know yourself until you isolate yourself from your ego.

In a sound, a moment or a raindrop now, anything can happen. The slightest illness can cause death. But I've seen so many stars tonight. I was lying on the ground. My hair grew wet with dew. My footsteps made no sound. My words turned to glass. My solitude to breath.

I can go now wherever I'm told to. Far, near, to vanished Epsilon-Eridani, to the mysterious cores of atoms or along Masonic pathways. I'll never lose my senses. Unless you've set aside your ego, you can't be really prepared. Full of meaning like the ancient texts, and yet indecipherable.

[The End]

Governor's House
Calcutta
January 11, 1973

On the occasion of the inauguration of Animal Welfare Week across the country, from 14th until the 20th of January of the year 1973, I congratulate All Lovers of Animals Society. A wholehearted and dedicated observance of Animal Welfare Week is much desirous for ending cruelty to animals and spread spreading information and awareness among the public for the improvement and upliftment in the conditions of animals.

Everyone knows well that we benefit from animals in a variety of ways. They are our close neighbours, and an essential part of the economic infrastructure of our great nation. It is unfortunate, therefore, not to mention in defiance of our religious and cultural ideals, that we are apathetic about them—and in some cases, even cruel.

I hope that observance of the Animal Welfare Week will arouse our responsibility and civic conscience towards those who serve our mute neighbours, devoid of the power of speech, and help protect them from the neglect and cruelty to which they so often fall victim.

A. L. Dias
Governor[*]

This is my last return to Calcutta. After this, I can go off to even another planet. For the time being, I'm coming from Mercury. With every push of the green light, my train dissolves the darkness and rushes on. The melted darkness drips down through the heat of the oxyacetylene. My tongue's dry and my blood's on high alert. I'm not awake on this long journey back, but I'm not asleep either. I haven't yet said how I'm returning to Calcutta! It's the same every time. Above the Howrah Bridge looming like two duelling giraffes, Calcutta is cordoned off by the Calcutta sky. In the middle, a *manhole* of a sun. I am a 5'5" dwarf, with coal dust on my glasses and a towel of smoke around my hair, returning to Calcutta. And this is my last

---

[*] West Bengal governor Anthony Lancelot Dias' address to All Lovers of Animals Society (1973).

return. Calcutta's roads are stuck all over it like *bandages* and *sticking plaster*. Calcutta's roads get run over by cars every night, along with dogs and humans. In Calcutta, the police-van *searchlights* catch people, their beams leaping forth like frog tongues. In Calcutta, the old dogs get drunk on drunk men's vomit, and when they look up at the sky to howl they see not one moon but three. And to ensure there's not the slightest difficulty in its armed efficiency, Calcutta is building an underground railway. The lumpen will hide in those dark pits like the farmers on Mercury. If there are knife fights in those tunnels, the sound won't reach the surface. If I keep digging underground, I will soon be able to dive into my earth's thousand-Fahrenheit molten *lava* and *magma*. Calcutta died a long time ago, but the lovely corpse cannot linger for much longer—let the furnace door be opened now. In the history of destruction, Calcutta will be proof that Herculeum and Pompeii weren't the last word. Calcutta's fate is grim. Because after my suicide attempt, and after spending some time at an asylum, I'm coming back again. I know everything, yet I'm coming back. I'm not afraid of counterterrorism. I'll pluck out of Calcutta's mouth its *Monument thermometer* and see how high its fever has run. Only I can understand the language of its delirium.

And I shall live as a *barricade*, live for aeon after aeon.

Whatever moveable and unmoveable property I possess on Mercury, I leave in your care. Give my love to that one-legged boy with the *crutch*. If you really miss me, look into the big toenail of his one leg and you'll be able to see me. To the black-eyed dogs, the ever-efficient spider, the *Negro*-song *records*, the transparent blind fish, the flowers of fog, empty booze bottles, water, scatter-strewn cigarettes, half-eaten dinners, paper, petrol, loverboys afflicted by awkwardness, lovergirls covered with tattoos, and the funny police—my counter-revolutionary congratulations. After the Green Revolution's success, those farmers who were driven into the pigsties by the terror of the wheatgrass and the insecticide-poisoned air—always remember them. The only ones not afraid of this revolution are the kulaks.

Just before I arrive in Calcutta, I feel a booming inside my chest. Anxious and eager, I go to the door, hold on to the rod at the doorway and hang out to see how far Calcutta is. As I keep looking, the wind blows across my forehead and there's a moment when sleep touches my eyes. And that's when it happens. Even after the head strikes a post and flies off, for a few moments the headless corpse stays standing, holding on. An ear, under a patch of skull with the hair still on, hanging by a bit of neck and skin right above the collar. The door is splattered with brains. The shirt billows in the wind. Only the head's gone. I'll gently loosen my grip and step down to pick up my head. The head has to be picked up, or the train can't leave. At least I can hop into the guards' compartment. And when, as promised, carrying my head in my hands, I reach the *coat*-clad ticket collector at the gate along with the others, will he not let me in?

The Murderer's Brother

Where's the road? Oh, brother, *murderer's* brother, our ride's coming to an end. There are no roads at night. Unless the strips of cloth binding the mouth of the city can be called roads. The lamp post sticks out like the hilt of a knife. Bloody *mercury* lamps, they've turned the night into a hotel. So much light. Then darkness once again. A city of murders and disappearances. Who orders so many murders, boss? Just the thought of it terrifies me. All you need is one heavy shower, and the *manholes* fill with blood and noise and light, swirling underground. Yet a light drizzle, and this same road glints like the muzzle of a gun. In the winter, it's hard to cut open the corpses. Clenched tight, like a lockjaw. The underground-rail tunnel, like a *bullet* hole. On top of it, as wobbly as a fractured collar bone, a rickety plank or maybe an iron sheet. A hollow sound as the bike goes over it. Don't fuck it up at the end, brother. People die when people kill, and when God kills they die by drowning or an *accidental* lightning strike. Chaand died trying to cut a high-voltage copper wire. He was hanging upside down, his face low, the current still sparking in the drool from his chin. Falling on the city, making the head spin.

'Right there. The crossing after the petrol pump.'

He shifts the gear to neutral, and brakes. Skids to a halt. I swivel my right leg over the bike and get off. Comb my wind-ruffled hair. I haven't been too long on the bike, yet it feels longer than the film. I have pins-and-needles under my *thighs*. I stomp about a bit on the road. He hands me a battered cigarette. Lights one himself. The flames shines on his rough face. He closes his eyes and inhales. Household burdens have made him give up all his addictions. Doesn't even go to the movies any more.

We hadn't taken anything, yet we were high.

'I'm off, then. See you sometime. Met you after so long.'

'Yes, so unexpectedly too. Maybe again at a *night show*.'

'The kind of shit I'm in, can't even go to the cinema these days. See you—'

'OK.'

Such is the end. It hadn't felt like this earlier, when he lied and lied about his brother throughout the film. Not even later, when we'd been coming back on the bike. But I couldn't stand the fuckwit any more. The motorbike jerks forward. He doesn't look back but does raise his right hand once. That's for me. A taxi suddenly comes out of the coal-store alley and onto the dark and empty road. The bike brakes and the red and yellow brake lights turn on simultaneously. The yellow light goes off. Only the red light glows. Fucker's flying it like an *aeroplane* now. The *murderer*'s brother, on his bike.

I'd gone to watch the girls and the *fights*. I saw the poster outside first: a golden-haired girl in a brassiere holding a gun, and a guy lying dead on the sand. A car parked some distance off. Seemed like it wouldn't be too bad. And then I saw that bastard'd come to the *night show* too. Another poster showed the girl and the boy standing beside a bed and *kissing*. The title wasn't exactly English—maybe it was the name of a place or something. Seeing the poster first, like this, is usually not a problem. Of course, sometimes they do disappoint, those films that are only full of talk. Even if there's a bit of heat at the end after all that yammering, it's barely worth the money. New

Empire was empty. I was buying a 75-paise ticket when I suddenly met him at the *counter*. I knew his face. His brother Lalchaand was in prison for *murdering* Milon. There's a close resemblance between the two. Although the brother's a bit taller. A bit rougher. He was wearing a dirty, white-turned-yellow *shirt* and black trousers. He smiled when he saw me. I smiled back. He'd given a two-rupee note, so it took a while for him to get his change. Then as we climbed up together, the way he hunched forward up the stairs, I thought I'd seen him parking a bike.

'I *thought* I saw you coming on a motorbike.'

'Yes. Have it two years now. A Jawa.'

We entered the hall and settled down comfortably in two seats in the last row. They were film *cutting* or something then. I had two cigarettes on me. I gave him one. His lighter flashed. New Empire may have raised the price of its ten-anna tickets, but smoking was still allowed. And if you sat in a lower row in the upper balcony, and saw some cuddling down below, you could still heckle them, chuck paper balls. We were too old for that now. He's got a brother in prison for *murder*. I've got a job. Accountant for a cardboard-box manufacturer. Boxes for balls, boxes for dolls, boxes for shindoor. I couldn't remember his name, not at all. Sometimes I thought he was older than Lalchaand, then again I thought he was younger. I think there was one more brother, if not two. I only knew Lalu. By face alone.

Newsreel. Ribbon cutting at some factory or another. Around 15 or 16 in the audience, in all. Even though there is no one sitting close to us, I lower my voice when I ask, 'How many years has Lalu done?'

In the dark, the light from the screen makes his face shine. 'Lalu's . . . three and a half.'

He leant his head back and fell silent. I noticed that he wasn't watching the film. A man stepped off an *aeroplane*. Someone put a garland round his neck. Then the sports piece started, and I saw that he was watching again. Rovers Cup *final*. He put his feet up on the seats in front of us. Right in front, a couple of boys weren't looking at the screen but bending over and peering at something on the lower *balcony*.

'Weren't you in Kashi-da's football club?'

'Yes.'

I understood the intent behind his question—Lalu had played there too. I hadn't yet realized that I'd made a huge mistake by letting slip Lalu's name. Of course, it was bound to come up even if I hadn't. Some time later, during half-time, he went outside but I remained seated. Because these seats are the cheap ones, they're never repaired. The walls up here are strangely smoky. Mouldy. Fellow's probably made a lot of money in today's market. Bought a bike. But hadn't stopped buying 10-anna movie tickets. Or maybe he hadn't made any money. Maybe he'd got the money in a fluke. Instead of smoking it away, he'd spent it on a bike. Actually, watching films for 10 annas is a matter of habit. In all the other halls, the 10-anna seats are the ones right in front. Only in New Empire are they at the back. And we've grown so used to sitting at the front that, now, from the rear, the screen looks tiny. He came back some time later with a pack of Bombay mix. Tore open the packet and thrust it towards me. I noticed that his wristwatch was old, probably his father's or something. His *shirt* was dirty too. He said he wasn't in *service*. But in business. *Spare parts*.

'Don't even get a chance to watch films these days. Looking after the household, the business—I've no energy left by the end of it. By the time I get back home, all I feel like doing is getting high and staying that way. Earlier, every time there was a good one, I'd be sure to watch it.'

'And now?'

'One or two a month—sometimes not even that. Used to watch the *English* ones a lot. especially the Westerns.'

We chatted about this and that for quite some time. The slides began. The New Empire music rang out. They've got a *music* just like the radio has, when it starts. I like him quite a bit. No one spoke much to them in their neighbourhood. His brother'd *murdered* Milon. Since then, they'd been outcast. The film starts. A riot of colours. Red stains, gunshots, and the opening credits. You can see from the credits that the picture's going to be a good one. I told him with quite some conviction, 'This one will be good.' He offered me his pack of Bombay mix again. Laughed and jiggled his legs. An incident like theirs had happened in our neighbourhood, too. A woman and her mother-in-law had accused their maid of stealing, and then beaten and beaten her to death. Then dressed it up as though she'd hung herself. Nothing happened to anyone. Since then their house is known as Killers' House. Their children used to fly a lot of kites. But no one would get into a match with them. The children from the other terraces would shout: 'Duokko, khuniyalko, ladenakko.' And if they'd dare to approach, the rest of us would quickly pack away our kites. It's the same thing that's happened to his house. The neighbourhoods were fairly close, so news travelled. His name's never come up, of course.

The white girl's probably the *detective*. It's obvious she's taking *orders* from the bald, white, cigar-smoking man across the table. A *Negro* took a picture of her the moment she landed at the airport.

Then a car parked on the side began to chase her car. A high-speed chase. The tyres screeching and skidding. The people who'd been chasing the white chick had to stop because a truck blocked the road in front of their car. I like watching films like this. The girl's hot.

'Lalu didn't *murder* Milon. They framed him in such a way that he got jailed along with the actual killers. Did you know about that?'

I knew well enough. Knew he was lying. His breath smelt of Bombay mix and chewing tobacco. I said, 'Everything I know is from hearsay. I wasn't in Calcutta when it happened.' Take that. I can play the game just as well as you.

'You've played with Lalu. Can he murder anyone? The ones who murdered are Jean and Binod. Actually, Milon's family was pissed with Lalu. They're the one who paid to set him up. Haven't you heard?'

'I'd heard there'd been some black-money trouble with Lalu. But why only Jean and Binod—lots of neighbourhood boys had signed up for the same racket, everyone knows. Lalu was not the kind of boy to get into all that.'

'Is that what they've told you? No one knows the truth, the *facts*. Won't tell them even if they do know. Everyone's passing on whatever bullshit they've heard. If you hear them, you'd begin to *wonder* if it was a girl matter after all. The girl from the Sarkar house, the lawyer family. Lalu had a *lovecase* with her. Later, Milon used to skirtchase about that house a lot. Then he had a fight with Jean and Binod over that same bitch. By then Lalu'd washed his hands off her. You won't believe it, but we were already looking for a wife for him. Fuckers, you fought over that girl, you died. But just because Lalu had a little case with her, you took him along too!'

I was astonished. The white girl's undressing behind closed doors.

'No one's told me any of this this. This is the first I'm hearing about a girl!'

'Just think! They're the ones who murdered Milon. Must've been some other shit going down as well. His family's all bastards. Their own son's going to hell, so let's screw someone else's. Such times— you pay, and someone'll even bring an elephant udder home to you and give you the milk from it.'

I knew all the *facts*. Everything that had happened. After the *murder*, when they'd released Milon's body, I'd seen it too. The white girl's lying in a bathtub full of foam, she's lifting her leg and the foam is trickling down the length of it. By my mother, that's a weird tap. No water, just foam. Looked a lot like the iron tubs from which the horses drink. I knew the whole case. There'd been a long love affair between Milon and that girl. Everything was fine. Lalu hadn't just *murdered*, he'd made someone murder. Jean, Binod and Moyna turned state's witness. They were the arse lickers of Bengal—for a few rupees only, they'll lie to this one and thrash that one to keep control. Who controls? Who doesn't? Would they've *murdered* if Lalu hadn't made them?

'*You've* played with my brother. Say, was he a boy who'd *murder*? It isn't easy taking a man's life.'

Shut up fuckwit. The white girl is getting dressed now. Hair's wet. As she walks across the hotel floor, something touches her foot. A hand, sticking out from under the bed. She holds the hand and pulls. It's the *Negro* who'd taken her picture. Blood from his mouth is trickling down his chin. Dead. They'd caught Milon at night, coming home from a chat near the doctor's chamber. A winter's night. Lalu'd thrown bombs. Two of them. The first one missed. The next one hit his leg and knocked him over. Then Jean or Binod *stabbed* him. He thinks everyone else is a cud-chewing cow. Bloody swine. I can tell him right now that Milon had uttered all their names in his *dying statement*. In the hospital, he'd lived for an hour or two.

'It's good that I have the whole story. I knew there'd been something fishy. In the middle of all this, Lalu's *life* got ruined.'

'Arrey, brother, what could I do? They framed him. If he hadn't gotten tangled in that screw-up, he'd have had a 2000-rupee salary today. He'd even got a confirmation from the ship company.'

I spewed bullshit, he lapped it up. We'd seen Milon's body. After he was stitched up, he looked smaller somehow. As if his belly was gone. Two yellow legs poking out of his chest, and this bastard is trying to tell me that his brother hadn't *murdered*. The white girl's legs were the best. I felt a little uneasy, then he started talking again. The white girl's running. Along the hotel veranda. Two men come out of the lift.

'*Murder's* great to watch on the screen. We're seeing so much killing, but all of them are really alive.'

I think Milon is alive too. But he'll only live once he gets out of the doctor's chamber into the foggy winter night. The *first* bomb will miss him. Smoke. If a bomb lands near his foot, any human is bound to be a bit shaken, whether it hits him or not. A few *splinters*, bits of ball-bearings fly into walls and windowpanes. The next bomb will rip the flesh off his face, lay bare the bone. Then he'll get the knife. Under his ribs, slightly to the left. Then a little downwards, in an L, all the way to the right, slashing the liver, the intestines, ripping his insides apart and then exiting. Through the smoke, Lalu, Binod and Jean, as though dancing. In the distance, someone screams. More screams. Running. Then Milon will give his *dying statement*. Tell all the names.

If this were a movie, we could see it over and over. We too could be seen over and over.

'The girl whom the fight was about, she's thriving. Got married last year. Got a great job in Bombay.'

'Set fire to it all, and now all safe and sound. Good line, no?'

'Just wait and see. God won't let her go. He'll do something about it.'

The whole film is spent like this. He talks about his brother again and again. Talks as if he hadn't been able to talk to anyone until now. As if he won't talk to anyone ever again. More murders happen in front of us. Daggers slice. Karate. Wrestling, kissing, dancing, a deep-sea diver with a glass mask. When the bubbles break out of the girl's mouth underwater, when a school of tiny fish peck at her, then on the *murderer's* brother's dirty white shirt and his weather-beaten face, on his nose, on his forehead, his eyes, the light shines blue. The smell of sweat. He's grown thin because of his brother.

'Used to smoke up earlier. I've left all that. And films, don't even get to watch them now.'

Who the fuck wants to know your sob story. The next moment I feel a little bad for him. What one incident can do to a person. Your brains've been rattled. You just don't know.

'The weight of the house is on me now. If not, there's so much I could have done. Now . . . I'm afraid somehow.'

In the end, she shot the boy she'd kissed and cuddled with. He belonged to the *opposite party*. And why shouldn't she? He'd shot at her with his revolver, too! They'd shot that scene so well. The guy, his *shirt* open at the chest and knotted at the waist. His jean-clad legs.

Even though he'd been shot, he threw his gun away, just to let the girl draw near. As he was dying, the white girl kissed him. The corpse, lying there. The End. Now two yellow legs will poke out of his stitched-up chest too.

I don't need the bus fare to get back home. As is usual after a night show, all the shops are shut, a few people in the dark, in front of a paan shop. One of them having a lemonade even though it's so late. He tells me he'll drop me to my corner. I tell him to wait, then cross the road and buy three filter cigarettes. Shopkeepers in those neighbour-hoods don't really care if you ask for a few and not a pack. He says he already had some. We light up. One stays in my pocket. He pushes his bike out of the stand, the rear wheel hits the ground. He sits, and throws such a kick. Once the engine *starts*, I sit behind him.

A breeze. Two and a half horsepower.

Oh *murderer's* brother, brother, *brother* mine—race these two wheels now, just enjoy! This is a film. The kid's good, though. A little mad. It's this madness that's saved him. Fuck, if we had some booze right now, it'd be divine. Belly full of booze, neckerchief loose, we got nabbed, with our caboose. Caboose means *chamber*. If I'd got a chamber now, fuck! I'd fill it with slugs and pop balloons left and right. Number one pop would be this brother's head. Crazy fucker. Faster, boss! Wait—let me grab the handle. When you'll ride your wife, she'll clutch you tight. Now it's your daddy enjoying the flight.

The motorbike picks up *speed* and zooms down the road in style. The cold of the night seems to have cast a spell on the three of us, the motorbike, the *murderer's* brother and I. I can feel, my hair's been blown all to one side. The zebra crossing rushes at us from afar.

Suddenly, beneath us, lie scattered laughter and parched rice. The zebra crossing recedes far behind. Thus I go back home with the murderer's brother on his bike.

'Mind if we go for a drive?'

'No, go towards the Maidan.'

The bike pierces through the coal heart of darkness. A police van. Picking up some girls. A bend in the road. Then round the *club tents*, and on towards the fields of the moon. The bike has no weight here. The girls are laughing. The *murderer's* brother is riding the bike. The *murderer* is doing time. We're totally useless. Our pockets are empty. That's why these *murder-shurders* happen. This flying motorbike, this dark Maidan, lights, the drunks screaming from their cars, Akashvani Bhavan, Victoria, Red Road—there's a murder in everything. A friend of mine died very strangely. The wind is bending me to its will. A cigarette in the mouth of the *murderer's* brother. The sparks fly.

That friend of mine, he'd been dancing in the waterlogged streets. A Qawwali record had been playing in the loudspeaker shop. The moment it finished, they played it again just to make him dance some more. And just then a lightning bolt struck him dead. If they hadn't replayed the record, he'd have been out of the water already. Smoke sizzled off his burnt face. When his body was taken away, I saw something floating in the water just there, like blubber. Actually, it's what I've been saying all along. We can be murdered at any time.

The road's upside down. Our motorbike's upside down too. The night city. The *murderer's* brother is riding the bike. We'd gone to see an English film. The traffic light at the four-street crossing blinks red and dark all night long. He says his brother isn't a *murderer*. But he's the *murderer's* brother. And I'm killing time with him. Actually, we're poor people. Beggars. But he's on a high now so he's burning a bit of petrol. A Chinese boy and a man in a lungi are asking us to stop. Why? Where does the moon rise with so much light? What is the use of so many stars? What does this city mean? To what end so much breeze when our breaths stick in our throats? The *murderer's* brother is riding. He thinks I don't know the real story. Cooked up a lot of tales in his brother's defence. But failed. He thinks he's found one convert, so he can relax now. His liver's throbbing with joy. But I know everything. But do I need to say so? I'll probably never see him again. The road's drawing to an end. The closed jewellery shop, houses, the girls' school, the wall.

He doesn't look back. But raises his right hand once. That's for me. A taxi suddenly comes out of the coal-store alley and onto the dark and empty road. The bike brakes and the red and yellow brake lights turn on simultaneously. The yellow light goes off. Only the red light glows. Fucker's flying it like an *aeroplane* now. The *murderer's* brother on his bike.

The motorbike moves farther away. His shirt billows in the wind and makes him look so strange from so far away, and it's so dark you can't see his head. Looks like a headless man, riding along on a motorbike. I take out the comb from my pocket, comb my hair. At my lips glows the cigarette he'd given me. Didn't let me watch the movie properly. I can't see him any longer. Only hear him because it's night. He's growing smaller, disappearing. Headless. The *murderer's* brother rides the motorbike.

I return. He's got me so used to the motorbike that it's hard to walk now. Fucking bastard.

Those Men at the Fountain

It's been raining nonstop for the last two days, which is why waves of floating moss and rotten-rubbish water from the open *drain* outside had come right into the shop and were now pushing at my feet. My mouth was full of booze, so I couldn't get the smell. Every now and then, coming and going like a school of fish, from the alley a wall away, the laughter of the girls standing there. I really like a girl from there: Phoara. Fountain. So finishing my pint, I was about to rest my head against the wall when a short guy mistook the water for land and, with a splash, fell into the *drain*. The girls burst out laughing. When I saw that the man wasn't moving, I tried to pick him up. He was quite heavy. I yanked him up and into the shop. Water splashing everywhere. On his knee, under a patch of peeled-and-wrinkled skin, I can see the white. I told the storeowner's son to fetch some lime. The man sat still for a while, his eyes closed and smiling. The moment the lime touched his wound, he frowned. Then smiled again. Then he opened his eyes, looked me over and said, 'Everything works out. Doesn't it?'

'Why'd you come to the booze shop again? You're slurring already.'

'Wait—isn't today the fourth? No one can stop me on payday. Didn't you see how it all worked out? I fell down, you picked me up. Nothing stays fallen for long. Not me. Not Khuki. No one. Everything works out. Let me get a bottle.'

Good idea, but he frowned again.

'It's nothing,' I said, 'Just the lime at work.'

'That'll work out too. When the skin's gone, there's lime. When the lime's gone, there's medicine. I've got medicine at home, you know. Lifesaver. They'd given it to my *wife* after her *operation*, to make the wound dry faster. But before it could she was dead.'

'That why you're drinking and lurching about? No one at home?'

On the way out, a huge towelhead tripped over Shorty's leg, wounded the skinned knee again. I swore at Sir Towelhead. The lime grows wet with blood. White under skin. Blood under white. And bone under that.

'No one at home?'

'Told you, Khuki's there. My daughter,' he said, and started waving his fingers in front of my face.

'What's the matter?'

'I'm talking to my daughter. She's mute. This is how we talk to each other. She's a very good girl, you know? Keeps the home shipshape.'

'So instead of drinking and rolling in the gutter, why don't you go home? Your mute daughter's all alone.'

'I go home all the time. Now pour. You've poured too much for me. Is it because I'm paying? Give it to me. I go home every day. My motherless and mute girl's at home. And the days are bad.'

The smell of tarka dal and the sound of laughter wafted in. A bus pushed its way through the water. Phoara's laughter could have overturned the bus. Like chopped onions, everyone in the shop was slowly turning dark, on drink and sweat and the light of the gas lamp.

'Who's filthy laugh is that?'

'Just some sluts. There's a whorehouse nearby.'

'Laughing? Women! Tell me, what's there in that laughter? Desire awakens. Then as soon as the bubbling's burst—nothing will be born. Khuki won't be born. Just my wife that had to damn die.'

'Where do you live?'

'Boral. Garia's the *last stop*. Stop for the last booze. That's what I've been drinking on the way. And sharing too.'

'I'm sure you work. *Service?*'

'Work?'

Shorty stoops. His breast pocket is full of money.

'They paid me today. Just this one day. Khuki knows I'll be late today.'

'The notes've got wet.'

'Eh? I should dry them. What say?'

The man grimaces as he puts his feet down in the water. Then reaches into his pocket and takes out some notes. A fat wet bunch.

He sticks each wet note onto the table top. I hold it down with bottles, empty pints and glasses. Customers come and go, stare at us.

'Boss, tried putting them out in the sun?'

He doesn't answer.

Three 100s, two 10s and a 5.

'This is all my hard-earned money. I've set aside some for my daughter. A 1,000 rupees. Not bad, no?'

'Not bad at all.'

'Actually, everything works out, you know? Just my wife that had to damn die. *Gall bladder*. Doctor said it was grown over. It was too late. At Sealdah, you know—she died. The doctor didn't take even a rupee less. Bastard! I'm a *service* man. Earn my own keep. Eat sleep fly the sheets high, balls're all you're left with when you die.'

'Quite true.'

'We're doing fine, you know. We go out, my daughter and I. When my wife was alive—'

Nyaba came to tell me that Phoara wasn't going to take it any more. She'd turned down two men. I told Nyaba to give her five rupees. Nyaba said his pockets were empty. I peeled off the flattened five-rupee note from the table and gave it to him. Shorty saw.

'—when my wife was alive, we'd go out a lot. We'd been to the Lake. Seen the fish under the suspension bridge. Such a *fine scenery*, no? Boats going to and fro. Then the Buddha temple. There's a special incense they burn there, you know?'

'Where's the temple?'

'Just beside the Lake. Haven't you seen it? You must. Then Dum Dum. Maidan. Museum. Aeroplanes—aren't those something to see! A month before Khuki was born, we went to the zoo. A white tiger cub had just been born. Did you know? So they didn't let us see the tiger. Then, the sea.

'The sea?'

'Haven't you been? Once, I'd got tips from a friend at work and gone off to Dharmatala, booked tickets for a bus to Digha. She was scared stiff! She'd never seen the sea, you see. I'd of course been to Puri as a child.'

'What'd you see?'

'Oh god! Just water, dear sir. Oof, what a sight that was! We had an amazing time. Have a look!'

'Look at what?'

'Our Digha photo! We had it taken at a studio!'

Shorty took out a tattered Rexine wallet from his pocket. Opened it. A dirty photo. Shorty looking quite good. No moustache then. A thin girl beside him. Khuki in her arms. Who was even thinner.

'How long ago?'

'Three years. She's been gone for a year. No, in fact it's a year and a half. I must be drunk. I've drunk a lot, haven't I?'

I was feeling very sorry for him. Didn't get paid all that much. And yet so much had been drunk away already. A mute girl at home. A wife that's dead. They used to go out a lot. I was listening to Shorty. Was I thinking about him too? Paresh, Jahar and Kashem arrived. They'd bought cucumbers, not booze.

'Who's this fucker, boss? Give us a fucking drink, boss.'

I was feeling rather magnanimous at that moment. All that money on the table, and Shorty didn't seem like he was going anywhere.

'Who's this brother, boss?'

'You really need to know?'

'What'd you say?'

I peeled off two ten-rupee notes, handed them over. The bastards went in. Shorty saw. The corner of one note was fluttering. At the touch of a careless finger, it flew off and began to float on the water.

'The money's flying, the money's flying away!'

'Just sit tight.'

'The money's flying away. Please, will you pick it up, my friend?'

'I am.'

'I should go now, my friend. Or Khuki won't go to bed.'

'Eat some roti and tarka.'

'I won't eat without Khuki. No, I'll go home now, cook some rice.'

Shorty peeled the notes off the table. But three notes less now, three notes that had worked themselves out.

'I'll be off then.'

'Has your shirt dried?'

'Oh, never mind the shirt. My wife's dead, that's why. Same shirt to work every day of the week. Ouch!'

'Is the knee hurting?'

'Will the lime cure it? Filthy water, after all. I think I'll use that that medicine, eh?'

'Yes, do.'

'You never said what you do.'

'Me? I do fountains.'

'Fountains?'

'You know, *exports* and *imports*.'

'Hey, Nyaba, you twat—' I called Nyaba. Jahar, Kashem, Paresh, and Binod, they all came.

'Help the boss over the drain.'

Shorty saw himself rising. Under him, dirty, black mounds of moss and rubbish-rot water. Shorty saw four bearers flying him across and then setting him down on the muddy street. Nyaba got off the rickshaw. The bastard'd really grown a mouth: 'Come on dadu, climb aboard.'

I put a packet of rotis in Shorty's hands. A *parcelled* pot of tarka. Khuki would find the tarka too spicy, so I put in some sweets too. And then, two tens, a five, and we'd drunk, so ten, and he'd been drinking and giving away drinks, so 20—I rolled up 60 and tucked it into his pocket along with a small bottle of red medicine.

'Friend, oh my friend!'

'Take boss to Boral. On the way back, collect the fare from Haren's paan shop. Keep looking until you find his house. Don't come back until you've reached him home. I won't need to whip you if there's any funny business, because there won't be any.'

'My friend, what's your name?'

'People threaten cops with my name. Best you don't know it.'

'Really?'

'Yes, really.'

Shorty was rolling to one side now. Any moment now, the tarka pot would fall.

'What is it?'

'Tell me you'll come again on the fourth of next month. On payday. You know, I don't drink any other day.'

'I'll come.'

Screech-rattle-ting-ting-ting the rickshaw set off.

'Friend, friend!'

'Boss, tell us now, who's that shorty?'

'Yeah boss, who?'

'My father.'

I went to Phoara.

You're sweating even though the rain's cold? Uff, sent over a fiver and now you're strutting about, no? Don't act like a cunt, Phoara. Eat sleep fly the sheets high. Why're you scratching your back against the wall, my dear? The hook of my bra's biting into my skin. Won't you come to my room? No, I won't. I wasn't there on the fourth of the next month. At the start of this month itself, the brownies picked me up, took me to their room. The West Bengal police wear brown uniforms. What happened to Phoara then? What happened to the fourth of the month? Khuki, look! Like the shadows of the metal bars, my fingers are telling you that I'm in jail.

Last Night

The gleaming wet road, the rusty tin roof of a motorcar-repair *garage*, behind it an old paint-peeling stunned-still old house and a *chimney* precariously propped up with haphazard wires—the sky can see all this. And, not as clearly, the burnt-black tin-backed shops and buses and the in-between blocks of darkness that were Matador sheds and not the half-rotten bellies of fish but the shells of banged-up taxis. There were crumbling and dead *accident* cars too, their mouths full of dirt. The sky view mists over every now and then, for it has been raining continuously.

Sad, angry raindrops hurl themselves onto the rusty tin roofs whose battered corners, beaten by the rain, crumple and break and fall in tiny pieces onto the floor or into the mud. There the water's turned red from the bleeding rust. The streetlamps are off. The insects that had slipped in through the cracks in the glass to eat some light, they were all dead in a heap on the floor. Water trickled down the glass of the lamp. The bugs' dry, dead corpses seemed to shiver at the touch of the cold water. It's raining nonstop. Not whining, but stuttering. It's almost one in the morning. When lightning flashes, you can see the ash on the garbage heap, the motor-oil-wiping jute rag, flowers, sanitary *pads*, discarded springs, coconut fibre, dead crows, puffed rice, boiled rice, fish scales—thickening into one wet mess. You can hear the banging of many empty tins, of congas and bongos and skulls when it rains like this. When it falls on bald heads.

But when it falls on flabby bellies or hair or hay, the sound is different. The colour of the water as it pools is different too. In some places a bit like ash, somewhere else like spit, somewhere else covered with a film of oil leaked from a car. Rain like this doesn't wash away the filth. The floodwaters push the burnt bidis and knotted condoms towards the drainmouths, and because there's water there too, and because there's black bubbles of *gas* rising from below, their opposing push sends them back to the street again. Where everything swirls round and round and then congeals into a stinking clot.

In the meantime, two boys are fighting. And every time they run out of steam, they sit on a car bumper or lie flat-faced on the footpath, panting, catching their breath, and cussing. If you see them from afar, you see two indistinct figures beating each other to death in the smoke. When the *headlights* of a passing car suddenly shine on them, their shadows across the walls of a house loom as large as a demon.

They'd punched each other so long their knuckles were raw. For a while now, they'd been staring at each other, panting. Their mouths hanging open, the better to swallow the wet air with. The tongues seeking out their own bleeding spots, licking them better. The one who was skinny and had a crooked leg, a punch had knocked off a tooth in his lower jaw and now his mouth was filling up with blood and froth. On the other one's face, under one eye, a gash in the shape of an iron ring, pulped flesh. The sting from their bleeding lips and faces was held off by two things: a lot of country liquor inside their stomachs, and outside, the cold of the rain. The high comes, the high goes, the push and pull makes their bodies slowly grow numb. At one and the same time they seethed with rage, felt sleepy with exhaustion, shivered in the cold, gasped for air. They'd come so close to each other in the scuffle they couldn't get their tone-deaf fists to even land a proper blow. Sometimes they'd rest their heads on each other's chests or shoulders and doze off. Catch their breath. Until they'd push again or be pushed away. Punch aimlessly. Sometimes land a blow. If it lands on the throat, it makes you gag.

The one who'd lost a tooth, he was weaker, one leg was crippled and thin. He was wearing a gamchha. His face was round like a potato, bloated, yellowish. He had a urinary infection. His eyes popped out of his head, round and large. A cockroach-nibbled bald head, a few wiry hairs here and there. Number two was a lot taller and wider, he wore a collared nylon tee (NO EXIT printed across the chest). Below, a pair of second-hand pants. Dark and dashing chap. The gamchha wearer was Lyangra, and the man he was fighting, fighting a ferocious *fight*, was Garib, although in the *motor* mohalla he was known as Garibwa. That dilapidated building that used to be a biscuit factory and that now sold hooch, and that everyone, from policemen to masseurs, from pimps to pistol pullers called Pint Mahal, he was a daily-wage earner there. Lyangra was a cripple, a birth defect—his mamma's boy from the moment he stuck a leg out of her belly. His father was dead. Not a full man by regular standards. On the other hand, Garib was an honourable man, earned well, ran the *body* shop at Chhedilal's *garage*, could do paint jobs too. He was a dogged sort of chap. That's why even though he wasn't a show-off, the goons never asked him for booze or bidi money. If he hadn't filled his belly with hooch, he would have killed Lyangra today. But its magic was such that he couldn't even pick up a brick to throw—the slippery moss-covered lump kept sliding away. And because his leg was crooked, Lyangra could never stand still in one place. Kept slip-sliding about. Hence no punch or kick could be properly aimed. Garib slipped and kicked an electric box instead, then sat there clutching his leg. Lyangra took the chance and began to batter his face and body with kicks.

The two men who are fighting so furiously are, however, friends. Pals for certain, maybe more. They were about 19 or 20. Garib paid for Lyangra's meals. For his mother Moti's as well. When there's the matter of the belly, there must be also a matter of the heart, also a twist in the tale. Garib and Lyangra lived with Moti. Slept with her. Garib was Moti's *lover*. To make sure she didn't get a child-wild, he'd had her fixed at the hospital. Although everyone knew the *case*, Garib's father thought that if he managed to marry off Garib, the foolish boy would let go of that old cow's body. Wife, mother, father—despite all three, that didn't happen. Garib carried on living with Lyangra. Spent his money there. Lyangra was his mamma's pet. Even his brains weren't fully grown. With his wide-open eyes opened wide, he'd simply accepted all this. It was only when he drank that he got mad. Then he'd either start to cry, or fight, freak out. This happened quite often. Garib would be better off if Lyangra died. But whenever he'd want to kill him, the hooch inside would make him so high that he wouldn't be able to finish the job.

Lyangra fixed his knocked-out tooth with his tongue, but, instead of standing straight, it now hung forward. He spat out some blood. Shook his head. Garib had turned his face up to the sky. His eyes closed, he was feeling the rain fall on his face. That's when Lyangra hit his throat. Garib fell, spread-eagled, on the taxi carrier.

Lyangra was winning.

'Going to drink your blood today. All your fuckery, your wham-bam, I'll end it all today.'

'See, Lyangra. You hit me so hard. Now I'll shove my leg on your throat and press, and it'll be your turn to die.'

'You'll kill me? Motherfucker, I'm a cripple so you'll lie with my mother? Disgrace me, and I'll put up with it? Fucking bastard!'

'Fuck off! Son of a bitch! Manslut! Who the fuck disgraced your mother? Don't I work my guts out? Don't I buy you food to eat?'

'I'll eat more. I'll eat your fucking life! Pour sulphur acid down your throat! Go to one of those whores, why don't you. Whoreson! Just leave my mother alone, man. Your wife's pretty juicy. A real *satis* piece. Go to her!'

During the day, when Lyangra loitered about the *garage* front, sat on the footpath and sang a qawwali—'*Parde mein rehne do, parda na uthao*'—then Garib would go out during a break and come back with two rotis and tea. They'd eat together. Then Lyangra would leave. Not forgetting to take a couple of bidis with him. Garib gave him money for the cinema too. The slum boys teased Lyangra, shouted 'Mama's brother-in-law' at him. He'd cuss at them, show them his dick, cry, chuck bricks, then forget his fury and fall silent. Sit on the battery box beside the paan shop and listen to the radio.

Grappling, they both fall to the ground. Lyangra tries to choke him to death. All the venom in his body seems to rush to his fingers. But he can't. Sinks his nails into Garib's throat, scratches, at most chokes him feebly and imagines the other one is running out of breath. If he can hold on for just a little longer, he'll be dead cold for sure. A sudden howling makes them pause. They struggle back up onto their feet. A few days ago, during a loadshedding, a taxi hit a dog, broke its hip. It now lay dying under an abandoned garbage truck. But its life force was strong, so it was taking its time. Slowly, slowly. It would lie there, drowsing, for hours, then suddenly the broken hip would hurt and it would let out a howl. Ants crawled all over it during the day. Flies sat. At first, the howl was loud and deep. Then, in the end, it grew high pitched and shrill and faded away.

The two get up and lurch over to the garbage truck. The dog can't stand up. Just raises its head a little. Dazed, rheumy eyes. Tries to wag its wet tail. The water streamed around his body and flowed on.

'Oi, Jongu! Jongu!'

The dog stares. His ears move a little.

'Feel so sorry for you. Want some milk and bread?'

Lyangra got angry at the taxi that had hit the dog. Sucking back the blood in his mouth, he shouted, 'If you fucker come around again I'll break your glass-fass everything! Man be, or animal be, they've also got a life like you! No one but God is allowed to take life away! What!'

Garib tried to explain. 'The driver was drunk when he hit him. Did he hit him on purpose that you're shouting?'

'Fuck it, oldie. The two headlights are to help him jerk off or what? Can he even drive? Just let me catch him one day, I'll shove the steering up his arsehole.'

'Jongu, look! Chhutki's calling you. Ay, Jongu! Jongu!'

Jongu doesn't raise his head. Just keeps staring. The rain is falling harder. For a few moments they stand there, silent, swaying a little. Then suddenly they snap out of it.

'Fuck it, he's dying.'

'If he's dying, he should go to hell quickly. Instead of howling and howling. If you don't die tomorrow, fucker, I'll put you in a sack and lay you out in front of a bus.'

'Yeah, smashed by a taxi to start with. Now a bus, a lorry maybe, they'll take him up to god. Set him free.'

'Die, Jongu. It's a rainy night. Good time. A lotta noise. Ganga water falling everywhere. Die now. God will make you his pet.'

'Yeah, Jongu! Please die now!'

The dog keeps his eyes shut. The broken hip has caved in and makes his rib cage look more swollen as it throbs with every breath. The rain grows even heavier. They both lean forward and look. They think the dog is dead already.

'Jongu! Ay, Jongu! You dead?'

'Jongu, boy! Yes, man. Bastard's dead.'

'Dead?'

'Dead.'

'We told him to die, and the bastard died! Then whoever we ask to die must die! Here, you die!'

'You die, too.'

'Ay, we're dead. See. Cold corpse. We're dead.'

'So send for a couple of *pints*!'

They laugh like hyenas and start jumping, splashing in the water. They start to dance.

'Jongu says Hari Bol!'

'Jongu says Hari Bol!'

'Bolo Hari, Hari Bol!'

'Bolo Hari, Hari Bol!'

'Words and wisdom, Hari Bol!'

'Words and wisdom, Hari Bol!'

'Mummy's tummy, Hari Bol!'

'Mummy's tummy, Hari Bol!'

They keep dancing in the waterlogged street. Through the rain, the streetlamps light up, one by one. They keep dancing, and with each kick from each foot, the light on the water skitters everywhere. A strange thrill has them in its grip. Makes them dance.

Two unpaved alleys ran diagonally through the slums and ended up on either side of the road, face to face. On the left, under a tin shed, stood Garib's wife, Maloti. Garib never went to her. The girl was dark but beautiful. Lined her eyes with kajal. Wore a white bindi. Dressed up. Always covered her head with the edge of her saree. Garib hadn't spent even one whole night with her. Never spoke even one nice word to her.

If he ever bumped into her, he'd clench his teeth and hiss, 'Go back to your father's. Marry again.'

'Ma's called you home.'

'Let them say what they will. I'm not going. Listen—take the bus fare from me. Take your clothes and the rest of your things, and go back home.'

'I'll drink poison one day. Everyone will know. The police will come.'

'Go ahead and drink. And if people know, let them. What's it to me? Police? Fuckers.'

'You shameless man! Am I not your wife?'

'Why are you, eh? Did I ask you to marry me? My father married me off to you. Brought you home. Tell that asshole to live with you, you're a nice piece.'

'You brute!'

Maloti had seen them dancing, leaping about, in the waterlogged streets. Lyangra was splashing the most. The wind blew the rain against her. It was growing stronger.

'*Disco* says Hari Bol!'

'*Disco* says Hari Bol!'

By the light of the street lamps, one could see petrol and motor oil floating on the water. The water had climbed up to Maloti's calves. Soaked the edge of her petticoat, made it lap wetly against her legs. Moti was coming down the alley across her. Maloti turned, began to walk back home. Garib and Lyangra's laughter rang out through the rain.

'Oy, Lyangra!'

'What!'

'You beat me so hard! Fucker, you hit me so hard . . . '

'I'm going to take your life, boy. The day, the night I get my chance, I'll turn you into a corpse. Shove a spike right through your eyes.'

'I've cooled down today. Fuck, I got so wet in the rain, I don't have any strength left. Or it would've been your last night tonight.'

They grope around in the water for bricks. Find none.

Moti walks out, slowly through the rain, comes and stands at the mouth of the alley. She's around 45. Gentle and lax of figure. Short and stocky. Big breasted. Her rain-soaked saree sticks to her, hangs low, close to her belly. There is an easy air around Moti's feet, waist, back and shoulders that Garib finds very hard to resist.

Lyangra spots Moti from afar.

'Ma!'

Moti steps forward a step.

Lyangra slips and slides as he runs through the water. He's going to his Ma now. Breaking his way through the water. Limping his way through. His gamccha comes off and drops to the water. Picking it up, Lyangra runs on, naked, to Moti. Falls down right in front of her. Stands up again. Moti wraps her arms around him. And Lyangra rubs his face against her chest, bites, cries.

'Ma!'

Moti kisses her son. His round, misshapen head.

'Ma! He's hit me so much. Look, there's blood in my mouth!'

Moti consoles her son, 'I'll give him a scolding. Come, son. Let's go home. See how late the night is.'

Lyangra cries, and, clutching his mother, inches along the slippery alleyway on his unsteady legs. The blood from his face keeps staining Moti's breast, then keeps getting washed away by the rain.

'Ma, you just wait. I won't let you be disgraced. Just you feed me some milk, Ma. And I'll turn him to a corpse.'

Moti kisses her son's face. Caresses him.

'You've drunk so much, my pet. Let's go home now, my darling. Come on.'

'Don't you let him back into the house! Just look, how much he beat me!'

'No, I won't let him in. Come, hold on to me, let's go.'

Moti is strong. She wraps her arms around her son, drags him home. The alley isn't flooded but it is muddy.

Garib watches them enter the alleyway, walk towards the slum. Then he begins to wade through the water, walks in the same direction. If he feels he'll tip over and fall, he stands still, regains his balance. His feet below the water feel light, his body above it feels heavy with rain. The way that Maloti had walked, he doesn't look that way for even a moment.

The rain falls even more heavily. Blinding rain. Cold wind, jubilant lights, darkness. The body of the rain, its gleaming front and back. Hairless. Jongu isn't dead yet. But he's close. The cold rain falls on his fur and skin and paws and broken bones, soothes him. Makes him sleepy. Even though the streetlamps shone, somewhere in the heart of the rain's clamour, the night was gasping to its end. The mad rain patters on the tin roofs. The rubbish, the filth, floats on the water. Whirling. Muddy water bubbles out of the jammed sewer grille. The sky can see no man.

So much water up above and down below, so much water carried by the night, now wet and heavy and swollen, as it heads towards a nameless, dateless, dreary dawn. Will this rain end? Perhaps nothing of note will happen tomorrow. The rain growls. Then again, tomorrow the third world war could begin.

A Piece of Nylon Rope

'When everyone had assumed I was ruined, from all sides, you see, *bad times* were surrounding me, and every time I tried to cover up one side, the other side spilt out, I mean, relatives, *friends*, *colleagues*, everyone, everyone knew that I was broke—right then, you know— of course, you don't know—I changed the whole *picture*, I mean, it changed—I suppose you could call it Providence—'

'Did you win the lottery like everyone else these days?'

'*Lottery!* The daddy of *lotteries*! *Lottery* is just cash and more cash. If your fate has other plans, can a *lottery* do anything? You know, a Teli guy in our neighbourhood, he won the Meghalaya jackpot. How puffed-up with pride he is now!'

'So, did you get a gem or a talisman?'

'No. Let me tell you. But first, is your date of birth a fifth?'

'Why should it be the fifth? It's a 23.'

'Ha ha! May I have a cigarette? That box looks real pretty.'

'Go ahead!'

'What's three plus two?'

'Five.'

'I knew it. I knew when I saw the car number *eight-two-four-zero*. Five, if you do numerology. Five's your lucky number. But do you know what? *Life's* like a kite. You think its drooping, falling to the ground, but the very next moment it's revitalized. You can feel the pull in the line. Meaning, all the other kites are gone. Still, no matter how high you fly, no matter how swift you soar, you'll have to always overcome a bump or two, never mind how lucky you are. Just see now, how my boy suddenly hurt his tummy. Doctor said there's nothing to worry, but we must wait 48 hours. Of course, he said he'll keep him a few days after that, too.'

'I heard it's a football injury?'

'He plays well, I must say. He really can *goalkeep*. A lot in that Tarun Bose's *style*. No fear at all. They invite him from so many places. Pay him to play for them. Feed him fancy meals. Just watch, he'll play Second Division next year. Very cool head.'

'How'd he get hurt?'

'Remember I said he has no fear? The way he picked the ball right off the striker's feet, the kick landed on his belly. The belly's a soft spot. D'you know what Bhaskar said when he watched his game? *Bright future.*'

The watch says one o'clock in the morning. It's been some time I've been talking to this man. I'm not disliking it, but now I'm feeling awkward. The cause of my awkwardness is that Lily had given me a *flask* full of coffee. But I wasn't being able to drink it. How could I drink alone? Didn't even have an extra cup that I could give him some.

Late nights at the hospital are not new to me, but it's been a while, so it feels new all over again. Raindrops speckle the car's wind shield. It's quite windy too. Stormy, almost. Out in front, under a *shed*, a young woman has been crying for a long time now. Sometimes snivelling, sometimes sobbing. An elderly man beside her. The girl is refusing to go in. By the light of the *mercury* lamps, the krishnachura and all the other trees, they look so beautiful. A branch of the krishnachura has bent over in the wind and is rubbing its face on the wavy asbestos roof. Torn leaves and flowers lie in muddy clumps on the road. The water sparkles on the leaves as they play in the night wind. The beauty of this light is something else. The Emergency microphone calls out someone's number. I see, through the rain, two sleepy people staggering over towards the ward. Maybe they need to fetch medicine. Maybe they've got the bad news. Maybe a white sheet has covered a face. Sometimes you never know the moment when they died.

'How'll you hear when they call your number?'

'You're right. I'll go wait there instead. What do you say? How will you know either? You've got a *patient* too.'

'I have someone there. My office bearer.'

'Is the *patient* your *friend*, sir?'

'Yes. He's had a stroke. They've released him from the Intensive Care Unit yesterday. He's getting better, I think.'

'I'd better go now. But you wouldn't *mind* if I say something, will you, sir?'

'No, no. Of course not.'

'I'm very scared, sir. Please will you walk me to the stairs there?'

'It's just a few steps away. There's a light there too.'

'I'll tell you later, sir. Fate doesn't turn around just like that. It leaves a little something behind. Like I've been left with fear. Look sir, look at my arm carefully. It's got goose bumps. Please, sir. It's not too far.'

'Come.'

'You won't lock your car, sir?'

'Oh, it's right here. Inside the hospital, so late at night, who'll do what now?'

'No, sir. They run a hooch business inside. The goonda *party*, understand? It's just as bad when you step out, sir. All sorts of women-shwomen roaming about. Just last night, three drunks had a fight over that.'

'Inside?'

'Where inside you mean? Right at the front porch, under that big veranda. That fucker guard, just standing and watching. Knows he'll get a thrashing if he complains.'

Our bearer, Dafaram, lay curled up on a cement bench. Though I couldn't tell if he was sleeping or pretending. The fellow was a very light sleeper. Night before last, he'd woken up Swarup right on time. It's been four days since Sanjib had the stroke. At office. His relation-ship with his wife wasn't too good. He'd been *drinking* too much for a few days now. Sometimes he'd say he was the *target*. Sometimes the *victim*. So far, it looked like he'd pull through.

The encounter with the strange man at least led to some con-versation. His figure is a bit on the fat side. His colour quite dark. Full-sleeved *shirt*, khaki trousers. And leather sandals. His glasses are crooked. And something I find quite irritating—he takes snuff. The only saving grace is he uses a kerchief to wipe his hands clean. Or he'd be wiping them on my car seat. His name is Jagadish Pal. Lives in Belgharia. Earlier, I used to meet all sorts of people. I enjoyed that. But now, my *life* is so centred around my office and my home that except for my visits to the market every Sunday, I talk to almost no one. There's a girl called Marjina. I buy eggs from her. Lily teases me about her. There's the fishmonger. There's the farmers who come from the villages. I quite like them all. In college, and before that, I was much better off. There was a nice *balance*. Never felt as though I was losing myself. So what if I didn't have money then? Many people feel like this. It may not be a new thought, but it's very true.

Thinking about Jagadish-babu, I realize I've never been to Belgharia. I'd heard it used to be a deadly place. Murders and maimings almost every day. Back in '70 or '71. Now it's all quiet. Like any other place. No matter what you say, all places now have a broken air about them. I could well go, one of these days. On my own. On the train, Ultadanga, I mean Bidhannagar, then Dum Dum and then Belgharia just after that. There, among a mass of uncountable unknowns, lived Jagadish Pal upon whom fortune had smiled. I was quite enjoying my coffee.

I lit a cigarette, opened my car door wide and suddenly my thoughts drifted to Jagadish's son and football. I liked football. But it's become very *violent* now. Everywhere in the world. Such a good team the Russians had, yet how miserably they lost the European Cup *final*. Dasayev had been at the goal. Inconceivable! If the Russians knew Jagadish-babu's *secret* for flipping fortune, would Rood Gulit and Van Basten have been able to score some goals? Does Jagadish-babu know about Glasnost and Perestroika happening in Russia? East Bengal's apparently going to get a *foreign player*. Jagadish-babu's son was a fearless *goalkeeper*. I'm feeling sleepy. Tomorrow night, it's Anil's turn to stay awake. He's our typist. A very nice chap. He'll stay up the Sunday night. The hospital will stay here. It stays here every day. I'll stay at home. I've never stayed at a hospital. Once, way back in my childhood, I'd had a tonsil *operation* at Medical College. The doctor'd told me to have ice cream. The rain's falling harder. Even a car can feel sleepy. Of course, my wife and daughter are asleep right now.

No burglar or *maniacal murderer* will invade the sixth-floor flat tonight. Suddenly, I thought that the fields—the fields around which thousands and thousands of people scream—the fields that were heard on the radio and are now seen on TV—even they're asleep now, they're getting wet. I rest my head on the steering. My hand is on the gear stick, as always. Then it slides down to my knee. I'm sleepy. The car is moving. The car is not. My vigil is over. I'm going back home. The lift's going up. Inside the main building of the hospital, the lights are yellow and dull. Or is it that they cannot glow any brighter in the heart of those ancient houses? Just one look at them, and you can't help but be a bit frightened. It's hard to believe anyone can come back from there alive. They've said at least 48 hours, and yet there's no fear in the man. I am full of fear for Sanjib, though. In matters of the *heart*, there's often an attack just at the brink of recovery. It'd happened to my brother.

The rain comes down hard. I shut the door, raised the window glass. The sound of rain falling on the car. I feel I'm arrested in an isolated and obscure situation. Stuck. I was nodding off again. When a light knocking on my window snapped me awake.

'Sir, are you asleep, sir?'

Lightning flashed. The man was getting soaked.

'No, no, I was just . . . Come around from the other side.'

'I'll come in?'

'Yes, it's raining—would you rather get wet?'

I open the car door while I say these words. Turn on the wipers once. No one to be seen. Jagadish Pal gets into the car. He's quite wet. He takes out a kerchief, wipes his head.

'Here. Have a cigarette. You're soaked.'

'I've had one, sir. They're expensive, sir. To take another one . . . I feel . . . '

'Never mind all that. Here, have another. Bloody freezing out there. Light up, enjoy. Light up, then tell me—that thing you said— *by the way*, any news of your boy?'

'No, they haven't called for me. The doctors were talking about a haemorrhage or something, that was around nine . . . but they told me there's nothing to fear. I'm not thinking about that. Nothing bad can happen to me any more, you know—I've killed off that path.'

Jagadish-babu lights up, sits quietly for a while with his eyes closed, then starts to cough, then to speak.

'The tobacco's a bit strong. Knocks you hard. I'm in a *private firm*, you know? Used to be owned by Swedish sahibs. Now the Marwaris have grabbed it. Our driver, Mukherjee, told me one day that all my palm reading and gemstones were to no avail. All useless. There was no place I hadn't been to! From that man in Behala who reads the palms of *film artistes*, to everyone else. Mukherjee said it was all fake, all lies. What I really needed to get was a piece of hanging rope.'

'Hanging rope?'

'Yes. Suppose someone hangs themselves to death. If you can get a piece of that rope and keep it with you, then boom!—whatever you want is yours. All the evil eyes on you, the vexing, the hexing—the whole fucking lot will vanish. Khoka's injured so badly. But do you see any fear in me?'

'Where'd you get it? Just the thought of it is making me uncomfortable.'

'You think I wasn't as well? My first reaction was being stunned. I told Mukherjee to help. He said, no it doesn't work that way. If you want something for yourself, you're the one who's got to get it some-how. That's how it'll give *results*. Visited a jail, and oh the humiliation. They laughed and laughed, said they'd stopped hanging people. Hardly any people to hang these days. Then I have a friend who works in Tollygunge Thana—a constable—he managed to get it for me. You know, after you cross the Lakes, you come to Lake Gardens? There some rich man's maid had hung herself. Scandalous affair. You can well understand. Pieces of that rope were in *heavy demand*. So many rich and respectable desperate for a bit. Would you like to see?'

This time it was my turn to be oddly frightened. 'No, never mind. I don't want to see.'

'Are you scared? Go on, have a look, if your mind is pure there's nothing to be afraid of.'

He took it out of his pocket. It was wrapped in a Mother Dairy packet. From the folds of plastic emerged a blackened, medium-size piece of nylon rope. Both its ends had been sawed off with some-thing, so they were frayed. Once upon a time, its colour may have been blue.

'You see? This is the real deal. But do you know what the problem is? Whenever the rope's with you, you can't be on your own. The minute you are, they come along and shout, "Return the rope. Return the rope." Can't you see the fear that's got into me? I can't stay alone at all. I'm with you, *fine*. The minute I leave you, the fears grab me. Just imagine, if she comes with her lolling tongue and broken neck and starts demanding "Return the rope, return the rope", won't you be frightened too?'

'And ever since you got this, your fortune's flipped around?'

'It's happening, slowly. You've got to be patient. It's the flip side of an accident, after all. The results ripen slowly. Once they die, you know, they become quite devoted. They want to do good to people. They've sinned, after all. The gravest sin. Now they let the good works rip. Someone's drinking plain water, they'll rush over with some sugar.'

'Couldn't you tell the difference? I mean, when your fortune turned?'

'Yes, yes, of course I did. There was trouble at office, trouble with moneylenders. They're going away slowly. My wife's health has improved quite a lot. How her indigestion troubled her—I couldn't bear to watch. I myself had a painful shoulder. That's getting better too. At home, you know, the rats would gnaw through the fences. That's almost stopped. My boy's name was published in the papers. But you know what—you shouldn't think about it. Leave it all to chance. Never ask for too much. See here, this car of yours, lay a hand on your heart and say: Had you asked for it? You should never ask. When the time is right, cars, money, respect, one by one they'll all come, you'll see.'

Someone's number was being called. The sound was unclear through the rain.

'Someone's number is being called!'

'Yes, they are. My right ear troubles me so. Let me go. Khoka's number . . . sir, did they say 52?

'I couldn't hear it clearly.'

'This time I'll go alone, sir. It's raining. Just watch me, sir. I'll manage on my own.'

Jagadish Pal gets out of the car and starts to run. Then slips on the mud and falls. I rush over to him, hold his hand and help him up. His knee is hurt.

'Thought I could do it without you. It's so muddy . . .'

'Come. Let's see whose number it was.'

We found out that they'd called out 27. Couldn't tell who the people were because no one stirred. Jagadish Pal sat down and rubbed his knee.

'Are you badly hurt?'

'No sir. But I'm getting old. Just a little hurt, and my head starts to spin.'

'I think you'd better lie down for a bit.'

'Yes, I should. They won't call any more, I think. Khoka's almost recovered anyway.'

'No, no, why should they call? You lie down. I'll go and wait in my car. If you need any medicines or things, let me know. We can go and get it.'

'All right sir. You—'

Jagadish stands up suddenly. 'I thought . . . I hope it didn't fall out of my pocket when I tripped.'

I came back to the car. It was dawn. When I left in the morning, I saw Jagadish Pal curled up, and blissfully asleep, one hand clutching his knee. The other hand clutching that pocket.

The next night, the Sunday night, Anil stayed awake at the hospital. Wondering whether I should tell Lily about the rope, or not, I end up not telling her at all. After all, she has a bit of a *nerve problem*. On Monday, at the office, Anil said that he hadn't spotted anyone who looked like that. The bearer came in a little later. He said that on Sunday morning itself, around seven, the boy with the football injury had died.

Deathgrant

Some people have such boring lives that, as they trudge and drudge through that boredom, one day they end up dead and they don't even notice. When you think about it, they remain vague even after they're dead. On the other hand, few are born as fortunate as I. Whenever I grow tired, some sudden occurrence or other is bound to revive me. But I can't tell this to too many people. My friends and relatives think that I'm scraping along somehow, just like them. Rattling about like loose change. Bunch of *brainless* sheep! Of course, it's best they think that way. If they don't, then they'll be jealous. They'll cast an evil eye. Envy tends to frighten me. And thoughts of the evil eye fill me with fear. The world is that way, I guess, filled with both good and evil.

The first thing I must mention is my incredible connections with the mad every few days or so. Whether probability or providence, it's bound to happen. One or two stray examples might help you understand, and not cause any problems for my business either. Still, it's best not to tell this to that female *psychiatrist*, the one to whom my wife took me. Just in case she changes my meds.

Just the other day, a man—shrivelled, wrinkled, like a flapperoo—caught hold of me. He had two fantastic *schemes*. He's sent them off to *leaders* across the world. So far, he's received two responses, full of high praise—from Thatcher and Gorbachev. He'll be meeting both. *Flying* out next month. Before I knew it, I was sitting down to listen to his *scheme*.

Number One is that he'll construct a *projection* from the balconies of *multi-storey high-rises*. A bit like a diving board. He'll make one or two right away, as an experiment. Later, when the government enthusiastically adopts his *scheme*, it will be a part of every architectural *plan*. He won't have to build them separately.

For the people of today, such an elevated spot for sitting or standing is highly necessary. No railings, and not too large a space either. It will be for those who want to live alone. People today are being hounded by so many things. *Chief ministers, scientists*, prime ministers—they are all hounding him. Even the *police commissioner*. As well as the SB, the CID, the RAW. That's when the *plan* had come to him. A sliver of space—outside. Personally, I was quite taken by the idea. Perfectly possible. But since I live in my one-storey family home, I don't think about it too much.

His second *scheme* isn't so much a plan—more a suggestion or an *adventurous proposal*, and bears an intimate connection to the first. He can stand, even walk, on the wings of flying airplanes. And he wants to provide first-hand proof. Such a sight will restore courage in the hearts of today's youth. The young need dreams, or else they turn to *drugs, cinema*, AIDS. He wants to do this on an *Air Force* plane.

Every plan is elaborately written out. Is accompanied by diagrams. Encased in thin plastic envelopes. All of them held in a *portfolio* bound up by string. He wants to know if I can help him with the second plan. That is, do I know an air marshal or someone like that. When I say I don't, he says then the least I can do is buy him some tea and a cigarette. I do.

I've seen many mad people like this, many shapes, many kinds. I've seen people who've been turned mad by nothing other than the shock of sudden grief. Seen my fair share of *suicides* too. Before they *suicide*, some tend to turn half-mad, apathetic. I've seen those too. Of course, I've seen not one but two cases where there was no hint of madness at all. Both used to hang out with tantriks. One went to Tarapith every Sunday. The other did deep politics at his office. Both ended up hanging themselves. Every one of these stories is true. The age of tall tales is over. Why would anyone believe me, and why would I tell them at all? Of all the madmen and *suicides* I've seen, a few were romantic *tragedies*. But now is not the time for stories about women. Although the story I will finally end up telling you, I first told my wife. That is, to a woman.

And at once the troubles, the tantrums. What about? That I've got to go see a *psychiatrist*. I'm a healthy-wealthy man, why on earth should I take off from work and go to a madman's doctor! Wouldn't hear any of it. Then her brothers arrived. All of them together dragged me off to a female *psychiatrist*. What a Botticelli affair! Just as well I went. A lovely woman. Almost foreign looking. And well spoken. Very friendly. I liked her so much that I ended up telling her all about it. Then, those tiny little white pills that she gave me, I've been taking them year after year, three times a day. Sometimes I take a bluish pill too. I grow bored. Irritable. I like the woman so much that I can't help trusting her. In my mind, I try to think I'm recovering from an illness. Of course, I have not been ill.

But what I am trying to say by saying all of this is neither about madmen nor about *suicides*. Three years have passed in the blink of an eye. I was coming back from Madras by train, on my own. Whenever I go on business trips, I have to rush about nonstop, from one place to the next. I travel Second Class on the way out, to save money. But all that travelling tires me out so much that, tempted by comfort, it's First Class on the way back. There was no one else in the compartment meant for four. I was enjoying the ride. Somewhere near the Andhra–Odisha border. Suddenly I woke up, and it was all dark. The train had halted. Pitch black. Can't see a thing out of the window. Once my eyes adjust a little, I see that the train has stopped at a small station. Dark-blue night sky. Against it, the shadows of small mountains or hills. A few lonely stars. People moving about. Torchlight. Stepping out of the compartment, I hear that a *goods train* has met with an *accident*. They have to move it. Repair the tracks. Then our train can carry on.

Suddenly, the lights came on again. I went back to my seat. And saw that, sometime in the darkness, someone else had come into my compartment. The man was definitely (not just possibly) a South Indian. His speech and appearance let you know that at once. He was probably in his 40s. Fair, *smart*, good looking. A touch of grey in his hair. A fine shirt, trousers, shiny shoes—his tie told me he must be an experienced *salesman* at some big *multinational*. I hadn't guessed wrong, but to this day I haven't been able to figure out what exactly the company was or exactly how big. It was so big it was almost mysterious, almost abstract.

After a bit of small talk, each of us lit a cigarette. Expensive cigarettes, he'd shared his with me. When I asked him if he'd mind a drop of whisky, he said he didn't drink. So I drank alone. No sign of the train moving any time soon. We both fell silent for a while. When the man spoke again, he startled me: 'Keep my card. Might come in handy.' The card was of velvety black paper. On it, in an unsettlingly bright yellow, was printed an address . Nothing else. The address was Waltair's. Nothing else, on this side or that. No company name, no TelEx or phone number.

'That isn't our real address, by the way. You've got to go through a whole lot of other places to get to us. But when you send a letter, make sure to have *your* address on it in *detail*. Our man will make sure he gets in touch with you. Might take a while. But find you he will.'

'What sort of a *business* is this? Sounds *secretive*, and *illegal* . . . but then you've got a card—*strange!*'

'Look, our company has *no name*. None. *We help people die*—gift them death, so to speak. The matter isn't *legal*—but . . .'

'You mean, you *murder?*'

'*Absolutely* not. *Murder!* Shame, shame, *we are not killers.* It is done with your consent, your *full consent.* A variety of deaths through a variety of methods. You can choose what you want, and *pay accordingly.* Want to die like a king? You can. Any sort of *deathwish*, no matter how *unusual*—we can arrange for it. Whatever you want, however you want it—you'll have it. But yes—you've got to pay.'

I had a long conversation with that man. I'm trying to tell you as much as I can remember. As much as my whiskey-intoxicated brain could grasp at that dark, nameless station in the night. As much as I have been able to hold on to for three years.

His opinion was that, for various reasons, each of us has a certain kind of deathwish within us. That is, a favourite fantasy, a wish, about how we are going to die. One might want to *romantically* leap off the edge of a cold mountain cliff one misty evening and plunge into a bottomless chasm. Another might want to be riddled with *bullets.* One might want to be set on fire. Another might want such a poison in their bloodstream that death starts with a light drowsing and ends with an ice-cold farewell. One might want to be conscious when it happens, another semiconscious. One might want to be strangled.

Another might be eager for the knife. Yet another might want to die on a pilgrimage, their ears filled with holy chants. But *wanting* isn't enough. No matter what you want, more often than not, deaths are *most uninteresting, drab and dull.* This company satiates that desire for death. Fulfils their *clients' deathwish.* Some of his words I remember *verbatim.*

'This has a *theoretical* side too. Our R&D is very *strong.* They not only look after the *practical* side of death—but also everything else—*The Tibetan Book of the Dead,* the Egyptian *Book of the Dead,* Thanatos syndrome, Indian death philosophy, from Abhedananda and Jiddu Krishnamurti to the latest murders, *suicides* and clinical deaths—they're working *nonstop* with all kinds of data. Forget India, nowhere in the *world* can you find this kind of business. Nobody else can even imagine it. I've heard there's been a *small-scale* attempt in Japan, but this isn't a matter of *electronics* or cars. On one hand they've got Toyota-Mitsubishi, on the other they can't think past Harakiri. The same bamboo knives, metal blades—totally *primitive. Not at all enterprising. Incidentally,* do you know which country has the most *suicides* in the world?'

'Probably ours.'

'No, sir. Hungary. The Magyars are extremely *suicide prone.*'

One can learn about many different kinds of deaths from them. No matter how complicated, how impossible the wish—they could arrange for it. A man in Delhi, his deathwish was a jeep *skidding* off a snow-covered mountain road. It happened. If your deathwish included a specific kind of disease, their *medical team* would look into its viability. But they don't cause the deaths of *other* people just because you said so. They would only help you arrange for your own death.

I learnt a lot from that man. Some people lead such dumfounded lives that even if they have a vague *idea* about their death, they are unable to express it. For them, there are a few set programmes. The most luxurious among them being 'The Record Player'.

An enormous record player sits in the middle of the ocean. On it, an enormous record, the record of death. It spins at 33 1/3 RPM. It's placed on a structure like an offshore oil rig. You get there by speedboat. The deathwisher sits on a chair placed atop the pointy bullet or lipstick-like thing in the middle, that pokes out through the hole in the record. The record plays an impossibly grave and sorrowful tune—Western or Indian. Rachmaninoff's *Isle of the Dead* or a woeful sarangi—whatever you wish. A few thousands of watts of sound slowly engulfs the person. As the record spins, they too spin into the sea, slowly fading, floating away beyond reality and illusion. When the record finishes playing, the pick-up, that is, where the stylus rests, enters the central, smooth, shiny part with a thunderous noise—and the force of it hurls the person away. They fall into the sea and die at once from the massive impact, their heads torn off or crushed. The moment the dead body hits the water, countless sharks race to it, drawn by the scent of blood.

This costs a lot of money. Very few can afford it. So far, no more than two or three have been able to listen to the Record of Death.

'Who are they?'

'Forgive me. But the *client* is greater than God Himself. We cannot *divulge* their *identities*. Of course, even though you and I are almost friends by now. Do you know how Mr __ died? You must remember.'

'How could I forget? That ghastly *plane crash*!'

'Plane crash, yes—but that's what he'd wanted.'

'But everyone else? Had they wanted it too?'

'Sorry. That's why this it's so ridiculously expensive. Because there are so many extra victims.'

'But they were innocent!'

'Innocent! My foot! We can't do anything about that! No one told us to kill them. What can we do if they insist on boarding the same plane? Moreover, this was his choice. Yes, choice. He chose. We arranged everything according to his instructions and his payment.'

'But why did he choose something like that?'

'Why? Because he'd removed Mr — in the exact same way. Lots of innocents had died then, too. That's why he'd wanted the same kind of death.'

'How many of these have you done?'

'Numerous. But why should I tell you all of them? Is it possible to tell you everything, or is it right? We do lots of things. We sell suicide projects. They don't cost as much. So much more. Just know this, that all the famous people who've died recently, from the machine gunning of the Bombay mafia leader's car to the suicide of the Calcutta film star—telephone in hand, 40 sleeping pills in the stomach, all, all of it was our company. And of course, there are the political leaders. Very easy to help them—all of them prefer heart attacks.'

'So you only help out famous people? I mean, grant them death?'

'Look, we're still establishing our company. Still some time until we break even. But yes, performance pride—that's our major capital for now. Later, of course, we'll have to think of the economically weaker class. To tell you the truth, it's much harder to deal with the poor.

Fuckers don't even know if they're alive or not, how will they think of their death? Not to mention that they're impossibly *crude!*'

'Consider those even lower. *Miles below the poverty line. Beggars.*'

'*Impossible! Last year* our R&D Department *studied* the *deathwish* of *beggars* in three *metropolitan cities*—Calcutta, Bombay and Madras. Their *findings* were . . . well, what can I say? *Silly and delightful.* Childish, even.'

'Such as?'

'The *image* of food came up in most *cases.* For example, to have their hands and legs and head and chest fill up with meat and butter and alcohol and eggs and fish until they exploded. They crave the alcohol. There was someone who said they wanted God to come down to Flora Fountain and lift them up in His arms. *Childish. Rather naive.*'

'But *imaginative*, I must say.'

'That they are. They're human, they must be. But yes, children, we get a lot of *valuable ideas* from children. Just a few days ago, our R&D found a *fascinating* story in one of the *American* newspapers.'

'What was it?'

'A boy, you see. About 12 years old. Somewhere near Chicago or thereabouts. Fellow dressed up as Batman. Was Batman all the time. Stuck on a pair of wings, and leapt from rooftop to rooftop. No one took him *seriously.* Even the girls laughed at him. A *child's* mind, after all. He thought: 'You didn't recognize Batman?' One day, he was found in the deep freeze, frozen solid over a few days. So many cases, you'll go speechless if you hear all of them. Batman! It's not that I don't drink. Go ahead, pour me one, make it *strong*. What's the whisky? Glender! Oh, it's a Scotch, I see! Never heard of it, though.'

I poured. For the *salesman* and for me. After a few drinks, he did a Batman and flapped off somewhere. I flopped into bed. The train was moving again. I could still hear his words—

'But, yes, the *grand surprise* that lies in death, especially in *accidental* deaths, we never *deprive* our *clients* of that *thrill*. Say someone has booked us to run him over with a car. But when, where, on which road he'll be run over—no matter how hard he tries, he'll never know. The virgin charm of *sudden death*—that remains.'

Who was that man? And what was his company? Deathgrant— can't dismiss the *idea* all that easily. I tried for three years to no avail. Secondly, don't we have, in each of us, an idea of death? And will that happen in this life, in this one life? Consider, for example, my own wish. That record-player death is too pricey. Of course it is! These are the doubts and confusions that I live with. If I take my medication regularly, I can keep them in check. If they get out of hand, then I pay a visit to that female *psychiatrist*. She changes my pills. Blue instead of white. Sometimes, during loadshedding, I take out the black card that man gave me. That unsettling yellow of the print is possibly fluorescent. The letters glow in the dark. If you get in touch with me, I have no problem showing it to you. Then you can write to them and see for yourselves. Might take some time, but they will find you. You can rest assured. Find you they will.

Toy

It's been a long time since Mithil and Mimi left Toy at home and went off somewhere together. They had no such plan, either. But Mithil called from work and told Mimi about the screening of Tarkovsky's *Nostalgia* on the VCR at Mahendra's. Told Amita-di to arrange for someone to be with Toy. The top floor of the small, three-storey house was uninhabited. The slender building had only one flat on every floor: Toy and his family on the first. Amita-di on the ground floor. And, before we go further, it's best we talk about the *aquarium*.

Last year, there'd been a huge upheaval at Mithil's office. Mithil's *Division Boss* had retired. A new man from Bombay had come in his place. He'd been with some Tata *concern* over there. The moment he came, the fights, the quarrels, the petty bickering began. Mithil's stress began too. And Mithil began yoga. Pranayam, Shabasan, etc. The chap who came to teach him yoga, he's the one who told him to get an *aquarium*. That man was a devotee of Sri Aurobindo and the Mother. Apparently, one of the Mother's texts said that watching fish in an *aquarium* calms the mind. Some people had tried it and the results had been quite positive. Therefore, the appearance of the *aquarium* as a form of treatment. Not too big. Didn't hold too many fish. Swordtail, guppy, angel, black molly, gorami. Later, a catfish. They kept worms in the bathroom. In water. But it was a lot of trouble. Hence, the dry food. Like Mithil, his son gave up watching TV and took to watching the *aquarium* instead. At the book fair, Mithil and Mimi bought Toy a book called *Multicoloured Fins*.

After reading it, Toy said, 'Baba, why don't we have a fighter in our fish tank?'

'No point. They'll just fight each other to death.'

'But the book says they don't kill each other. They just tear off their fins. And those regrow.'

'You read that?'

'Yes. Do you know what the scientific name of Angel is?'

'What?'

'*Pterophyllus emekei.*'

That evening, Mimi explained in detail to Toy what he should do, hour by hour. He should be a good boy and drink his Complan at seven. *Fruit* custard at night. Besides, there might even be a *surprise* for him later, when they got back. There was nothing for children on TV. It would have been good if there were. Toy should drink his Complan and then sit to study. Amita-di would come at eight to check in on him. The durwan would keep an eye on him too. If a stranger came, the durwan would tell them to visit later. Not that anyone was meant to come. And Mimi and Mithil would be back by 9:15 anyway. Of course, Toy was such a calm, well-mannered, and quiet boy that both Mimi and Mithil knew that there was no need for worry. Mimi boarded a minibus from in front of the house. Toy waved at her from the veranda. It was quarter to six. Mahendra lived four *stops* away.

Toy stood on the veranda for a long time and counted cars. Played that game. Summoning cars as he wished. It wasn't too cold yet. Though the sun was setting earlier, and there was a hint of fog around the streetlights. The Summoning Cars game had been invented by Toy himself. No one but he knew about it. *An Ambassador is going to come now.* It did. *One–nil. Now a Maruti.* But it was a police van. *One all. A Maruti again.* Maruti *two to one.* Cycles, two-wheelers, buses and mini buses—the game didn't include those. The lights were glowing in all the three rooms in the flat. With a 45–37 victory, Toy went back in to drink his Complan. Five past seven. Mithil and Mimi called at quarter past.

Is everything all right?

Yes.

You aren't afraid, are you?

No.

Finishing with the five-problem math homework would be enough for the evening. He could practise handwriting tomorrow morning. Toy put the phone down, and sat down with his sums. The last one was quite protracted and tough. Lots of multiplications and divisions. And it was during this last problem that the bell rang: Amita-di!

'What are you doing, Toy-*babu*?'

'I'm finishing up my homework. Math.'

'I've never seen such a good boy. You're not afraid, right?'

'Not at all.'

Amita-di gave Toy four Hajmola *candies.* He kept two on his desk and two on his parents' *bedside* table. He couldn't find the solution to the math problem. It was ten past eight.

Toy went to the bathroom and peed. Pulled the flush. Then climbed onto the commode and opened a box attached to the wall that would've been out of his reach from the floor. A wonderful smell wafted out. A mixture of eau de cologne and after-shave lotion all together. Whenever Mithil went on tour, he took along a small, incredibly *cute miniature* heater to warm his shaving water. Toy brought that down.

Mithil and Mimi came back home at exactly half past nine. They found Toy attentively watching TV. A live *programme* on the cable, Pink Floyd in Australia: psychedelic lights, smoke, waves of long hair flying about in *slow motion*. Bright lights like bolts of lightning bounce off the blue guitar. They'd brought some ice cream for Toy. Toy had it for dessert instead of the *fruit* custard. Then he went to bed. Mimi, chatting with him in bed, had also dozed off a little. Mithil was still wide awake. He felt candles from *Nostalgia* burning around him. Such dedication to keep a candle lit . . . Mithil felt his restlessness returning. Perhaps he should have a smoke, and sit and watch the *aquarium* for a bit.

The *aquarium* light is on. Its small tin lid open, and a pencil lies diagonally across the top. From it, dangles the small immersion heater. The fish are all dead.

Because of the immersion heater, an invisible convection current had been produced in the water, and the warm water was rising and the cool water descending, and in that invisible current the fish rolled about and bobbed from side to side. The water was quite hot. The submerged doll's mouth was open, belching silver bubbles. Little bubbles also rose from the side of the immersion heater.

Toy didn't go to school the next day. His parents took him to a *psychiatrist*, Dibyendu Mukherjee. He was known to Mimi's uncle. Mithil and Mimi sat outside while Dr Mukherjee spoke to Toy for almost an hour. When he finally emerged, Toy was holding an Amul chocolate and both he and the doctor were beaming.

'Mr Toy, you sit here and read this book. I need to talk to your parents, OK?'

Toy nodded. Dr Mukherjee said, 'Oh, what a lovely chat we had!'

Back in his chamber, Dr Mukherjee told Mimi and Mithil: 'As *macabre* as the incident might seem to you, I don't think it's anything very *serious*. When I talked to him, what really *impressed* me most about your boy is that there's not a hint of *aggression* in him. Such a sweet, calm mind . . . I recommend that you *ignore* the whole matter. This isn't a problem. *He is perfectly normal. It's a sort of curiosity . . . almost scientific.'*

A few days after this incident, Mithil read in a foreign paper an article about a few homicidal children in England and France. The news had led to heated debates. A large section of French psycho-analysts had said that the cool-headed and cold-blooded way in which the children had described their crimes, it seemed as though they were not entirely devoid of a scientific mentality.

Mithil made Mimi read it too.

Toy's parents no longer had anything to worry about him.

Old Kahar's Fortune

The young schoolmaster comrade shouts over the noise of the jeep, 'What Kahar did you say?'

Anil-babu had been dozing, 'Eh . . . did you say something?'

'What Kahar did you say?'

'Old—Old Kahar,' says Anil-babu and nods off again.

During the *election campaign*, Anil-babu hadn't been able to visit Gobodh in *south-west* Harinbari even though he had really wanted to. *They* had, though. With a truckload of brand-new cycles, clothes, *flood-relief* milk from the breasts of foreigners silently removed from the aid packages and heaps and heaps of posters. Yet, they'd lost. They had to push for better roads now, and for that an *Assembly candidate* was more necessary than a *Parliamentary* one. Such thoughts made the schoolmaster's mouth run dry, his tongue feel heavy. Yesterday, there'd been a *reception* at the grand Rabindra Mancha. Today, they were going to Gobodh. And this evening itself, Anil-babu would probably take the rocket-bus and return to Calcutta—and after some talks there, go on to Delhi. Were they filling air because the tyres were flat? A hired jeep. Ramshackle. Some black-marketeer's *side business* in the city. Of course, he was charging no more than the cost of the petrol. This just in: In Harinbari's Lok Sabha constituency, Left Front–supported independent candidate Anilchandra Mukhopadhyay is ahead of his closest rival, the Janata Party's Bashishtacharan Das, by more than 60,000 votes . . .

Anil-babu. Yes, that very Anil-babu, the legend of the Tebhaga movement, that Anil-babu was now making a political comeback. The red *flag* fluttered atop the jeep. The schoolmaster comrade liked the name a lot—Old Kahar. Anil-babu's farmer comrade from '46. Everyone other than Old Kahar knew that if he hadn't been forced into standing for elections, and if the Calcutta headquarters had not put pressure on the district level to have him do so, none of this would have been possible. He is the one to whom Anil-babu is going right now. A herd of cows splits in two and scurries away on either side of the road. A calf freezes in confusion, not knowing which way to go. The jeep slows down.

A bare-chested Bengal farmer. A truck-smashed now-dried dead snake on the road; the jeep runs over it again and rushes on. These belts have always been very *violent*. The jeep jerks suddenly, and the schoolmaster's head bumps into its canvas roof. He casts a worried look at Anil-babu but Anil-babu is unperturbed. He needs Old Kahar. Gobodh's Old Kahar. The Gobodh–Mohishbodh *belt* had been an impenetrable stronghold during Tebhaga. The number of police that returned was far lower than the number that went in. Of course, these were more or less local legends. And old people tend to exaggerate, whether they're speaking or writing. A bus was coming from the other side, so the jeep swerved. A cloud of dust filled the space. If Anil-babu raised one hand, ten thousand lathis would be raised in support . . . Even the women in the villages would rush out with their botis and axes . . . *We want Tebhaga* . . . Back then, Anil-babu could easily walk 20 miles . . . And he had that *sixth sense*, so essential for survival . . . All the detective reports were turned topsy-turvy . . . *We want Tebhaga* . . . As soon as the swarm of arrows flew at them on the fields of Gobodh, the police were forced to retreat . . . it was night then, so the first few arrows had their heads wrapped in cloth and set aflame . . . Eight bodies fell, red flags clutched in their hands . . . The police couldn't snatch the corpses, though . . . The dhamsa drums keep beating, the torches glow and the corpses are laid out at the heart of the village . . . Muffled sobs . . . This just in: In the Harinbari Lok Sabha constituency, Left Front–supported candidate Anil-chandra Mukhopadhyay has defeated his closest rival Bashishta-charan Das by more than a 1,20,000 votes. The security deposits of three independent and one Congress candidate has been forfeit . . . Eight bodies burn on the banks of the muddy river . . . and Old Kahar's eyes sting from the smoke of the blazing logs . . . the five villagers burning . . . along with his brother and his two sons. We want Tebhaga.

The garlands have been lying on the seat beside the driver since last night. Turning off from the highway to the city, the jeep goes down and along a sloping grassy path for a while and then onto another paved road with the muddy river alongside. So this is how it was. Ever since infrastructure has been made a priority, the look of these places has changed entirely. The National Highway bounds along before the eyes of the hungry cows and villagers. Electric towers shoot up into the sky. If the muddy river looked like this the whole year through, then the word 'relief' would become redundant. But the muddy waters of the muddy river can coil its currents around people and buildings and trees, swallow them whole, overflow its banks and flood everything.

As you know, through the sustained struggle of the common man, the strongholds that have emerged among these starving and helpless farmers are unbreakable and extremely powerful. Thousands and thousands of people came to our meetings, cast their vote for us. They came to see us, to hear us. We can proudly say that we did not bring them with the threat of guns or goons, nor did we force them or trick them. They came voluntarily, because they wanted to. We didn't send lorries. We didn't send buses. They came because their ideals and our politics are one and the same. Comrade, I believe this is progress. We progress every day. We move forward! This is why my victory that I celebrate today is not an extraordinary occurrence . . .

Early in the morning, you can sometimes see the mountains against the sky . . .

Anil-babu often recalls a particular scene. After his exams, he'd go home to his village. Got out his bicycle and set off for a ride. Up to Pagoltara, and back. He'd seen the mountains sparkle in the early morning sun. He'd seen them again as well, but that one morning's glimpse is the one he remembers the most. That was the year he met Charu Majumdar at Moynaguri. The jeep brakes with a screech . . . the pitch road slopes down for a bit and then splits in two. The driver was about to ask a girl carrying a baby the way to Gobodh, but Anil-babu glanced at the muddy river once and told him to go left. Left . . . left . . .

The jeep bounces along uneven paths. The soil here is hard, the ditches and potholes feel like rock. The first car to come here was probably a police vehicle. But ever since they dug the trenches, they hadn't returned. Some of the *spies* knew the secret routes, but they always cautioned the police against this road in particular. 1946—the tenant farmer must give a third of his crop to the landowner. Old Kahar . . . Panjiya, Nalatbari, Moubhog. One hundred and twenty-one rounds were shot at Khanpur. Twenty-two were killed. And in the fields of Gobodh, the torches blazed in a circle around the eight dead—all night—Old Kahar's two sons and brother . . . The dhamsas drummed all night . . . and those wailing songs . . . As soon as he enters Gobodh, Anil-babu sees the Left Front's slogan painted over the huge Cow-and-Calf festoons, over the posters of the other parties, over roadside *signs*, over the earthen walls and bamboo fences. Peeking through a *poster* of Indira Gandhi's face, Anil-babu spots his own name.

The boy doesn't understand, and calls out to his uncle. Meanwhile a crowd gathers around the jeep. His uncle namaskars Anil-babu, sends off the older thin-legged, stick-clutching boy to inform Old Kahar, but doesn't move an inch himself. The crowd thickens, trying to get a glimpse of the Lok Sabha member. These people don't even get to see an MLA first hand, let alone an MP. The entire village gathers around him. Anil-babu keeps his hands pressed together, keeps doing namaskar. Two middle-aged people touch his feet and tell him their fathers' names . . . I've heard so much about from my father, sir . . . Anil-babu recognizes them easily.

'Why make Old Kahar come all the way here? Come, why don't we go to him instead?'

Women come out from the low houses and Anil-babu namaskars them as well. The children stare agape at even the jeep driver; the grown-ups shoo them away. The schoolmaster comrade is overwhelmed with all the attention.

'You've travelled such a long way! Please, have something to eat and drink.'

'Maybe later. I'd like to meet Kahar first. I wonder if he remembers me.'

Humans never forget. Kahar had left out a line last night, to catch snakehead fish—a line and hook trap. Fish hadn't taken the bait, though. The hook had got stuck in something, perhaps a tree trunk. Kahar was in the water, treading his way forward, past the snail shells and sharp metal bits. He had no one left but his younger son's wife. The son had taken another girl and run off to the city. Kahar stands in waist-high water. The thin-legged boy shouts from the water's edge: 'Dadu, dadu! A city babu's come. He's looking for you. Looking for Old Kahar.'

'A city babu? Police?'

'No, not police. The old man who's won the vote. He's come to see you. In a car.'

'Oh god! The big-babu—Anil-babu is here!'

In his hurry to get to land, Kahar slips and falls face first into the water. His spiky white hair and beard—even his white eyebrows—are soaked and lie flat against his skin. Kahar can't see well. The eyes inside those sockets are grown dull—what is blurry in the day is almost invisible at night. He gets out of the water. The boy asks, 'Dadu, won't you dry yourself?'

'The wind'll dry me off. Come on, let's go.'

The veins on his forehead are swollen, his skin entirely wrinkled. When he takes a deep breath, his ribs threaten to burst through his back. As soon as he passes his courtyard, Kahar comes face to face with a crowd.

Humans never forget.

Anil-babu stoops a little. 'How are you, Kahar?'

'How are you, Raja-babu? I'm like this—I'm alive.'

Kahar bursts into tears and the two men embrace. Anil-babu's clothes grow damp from the still-wet Kahar. Kahar pulls Anil-babu's face close and stares into his eyes.

'I knew this would happen. It must happen! Everyone other than Firman's household and his bitches voted for you.'

'Firman . . . you mean Daulat's boy? Is Daulat alive or dead?'

'Dead—but what's the difference? He's left Firman. Firman's still left.'

'His father gave us a lot of trouble. We must change everything now. Everything will change. All right, Kahar? We never had this much power before. It's an absolute victory. It'll take time, though. This is not the time for haste. Am I right, Kahar?'

'Let me show you something, Raja-babu. Come. No one knows about it.'

Some of the others try to follow but Kahar doesn't let them.

'No one but Raja-babu is going to come,' he says. And they take a step back, and watch his antics.

'Come on, come. Don't step in the mud.'

Mud and ash. Mixed with rice starch and rotting weeds. Kahar pulls Anil-babu to the pond behind the house. Then with a broken iron blade, he scrapes away some of the ash-mud on the ground to reveal a rotten panel of wood. Kahar beats on it a few times to loosen it, then when the ash-mud crumbles a little, he lies down flat and plunges his hand into a hole in the ground and pulls out the lower edge of a mud-covered object. The butt of a gun, the wood rotten and full of holes. One could hear a scraping inside it, and when Kahar banged it on the ground a few times, the termites fell out and scurried away. The muzzle is full of mud, there's mud all over its body.

A *musket.*

'There are cartridges too . . . Ten of them, further down. I didn't hand it in, Raja-babu. I'll hand it in the day you rule. Firman doesn't know. Thinks he's got the only gun in town. Just say the word, and I'll go crazy again. I don't have anyone, after all. People say Kahar's crazy.'

'Is this one of the three stolen guns?'

'So what? It is. Do you want it?'

'No, Kahar. You'd rather keep it hidden. To tell you the truth, we're not in power yet.'

'Then what was this? What did Raja-babu win?'

'I won the election. What if I lose next time?'

Old Kahar can't understand so much. His chest is covered with ash and mud, he looks like Shiva. He puts the gun back into the ground. Sweeps ash and dirt onto the wooden board again, stomps on them until the board is totally hidden from view.

'I have no one, Raja-babu. And I've seen my fair share of corpses. I have no will to live any more. Two sons, brother—they got shot. No wife, no one. This one is the younger fellow's wife. What do I do?'

'What can you do, Kahar? Stay alive. You *must* stay alive. Do you remember those days? You've got to stay alive on the strength of that. What do I have either, tell me?'

Perhaps the memories come rushing in, for Old Kahar starts to cry. Everyone watches. Someone brings enamel cups full of jaggery-sweetened tea. Kahar's house leans to one side, slopes towards the pond at the back. Anil-babu shares the tea with everyone. The leaf-thatched shade is torn and tattered.

The time for Anil-babu's departure draws near, and he namaskars everyone again. Old Kahar trudges along beside him. The thin-legged boy walks beside him too, as does everyone else. On one of their heads is being carried a large jackfruit. Old Kahar had grown four huge ones. Two had been stolen by the Guo sons. One, Kahar will take to market to sell tomorrow. It was then that the incident occurred. And it is that incident that will be the appendix to this tale.

Putting the jackfruit in the jeep, Old Kahar spotted a basket inside. Containing four large pineapples and two more jackfruits. And Nalish, wearing a lungi and kurta, laughing and smoking with the driver. Kahar asks, though he knows the answer: 'Whose basket is this?'

Nalish blows out some smoke: 'Firman Ali's gift. New MP's visiting the village. So the village master has sent his regards.'

Nalish namaskars Anil-babu: 'Don't forget about the station, sir. The blessings of the village will be upon you.'

Kahar's words drown everything else: 'Firman! Comrades don't take gifts from blood-sucking land owners! Throw them out!'

Nalish: 'An insult to Firman is an insult to this village. Watch your tongue, old man.'

The schoolmaster loses his temper: 'Whom did you call the village master? We have no masters. Are you threatening us with talk of masters?'

'I'm telling you, throw it out!' Kahar shouts again.

No one steps forward.

Kahar throws out the basket. Pineapples and jackfruit roll on the ground. 'Firman's fruit has no place here. It's the fruit of destruction, of death.'

Nalish doesn't say another word but speeds off on his cycle. The crowd parts to make way for him.

Anil-babu bids Kahar farewell and gets into the jeep.

'It's absolutely right of you to lose your temper. If there's any trouble, send word to the city. People aren't to be trusted.'

'Yes, come to us,' the schoolmaster says, 'If you say Amulya at the party office, they'll know who you're looking for.'

It was needless to say that no one would recognize him if he said 'Old Kahar'.

The jeep drove off billowing fumes of burnt petrol, bouncing over the hard, rock-like ground. The people of Gobodh waved at the jeep, even Old Kahar and the thin-legged stick-wielding boy. In the distance, a cloud of dust and the jeep slowly disappears.

A continuous rattling sound.

'Come, let me have one of those cigarettes of yours.'

The schoolmaster hurriedly takes out his Charminars and matches.

'You smoke?'

'Not really. A puff or two now and then. It's an addiction, after all. Why add one more?'

Anil-babu balls his hands into a fist around the cigarette and takes a deep drag. The road back always ends quickly. Suddenly he feels he'll never see Old Kahar again. He'll go to Calcutta, to Delhi and goodness knows where else. So many discussions, so many papers, so much work. And somewhere far away, a thousand miles away, in a dark field, Old Kahar will clutch the dirt-jammed rifle and the ten useless cartridges he'd stolen 30 years ago and stand guard over the corpses of his sons, his brothers and his friends. The fireflies will glow. The fireflies will die, pricking the darkness with light. The muddy river will heave and swell and flood its banks. And on those waters will fall the light from the burning pyres. By the river, by the eight pyres, Old Kahar will sit for age after age. They'll never see each other again. Anil-babu felt a pang of sorrow. He wanted to turn the car around, go back to Kahar and talk some more. What's the use of going to Delhi? And couldn't he say they were a martyr family, couldn't he arrange a monthly allowance for them? Anil-babu decided he'll do just that. Kahar's life was hard indeed. The jeep comes to the fork in the road, gets back onto the pucca stretch and races along towards the city. The flag atop the jeep flutters in the wind.

It rained that night. All the world's mud seems to be stuck to their feet. A huge crowd, people from eight or ten villages selling their wares. There's a sharbat cart filled with green and yellow bottles, surrounded by a crowd of children. Some other had come from the city to sell government lottery tickets. They played songs on battery-powered loudspeakers; the boys sang along.

> 'Bombai se aaya mera dost,
> Dost ko salaam karo.'

> 'My friend's come from Bombay,
> Greet him all!'

They come like tigers on the prowl, and the girls scatter and flee. Mud from their feet splashes onto their own faces. They grab a woman by her chest, claw at her as she struggles and her little son cries out in fear. Then they let her go. They pick fruits from the stalls at will, take

only a bite and then throw them back into the baskets. Their fore-
heads are dotted with shindoor, their reek of cheap liquor—Nalish,
Anwar, Kartik, Kochey and Pakhot—they surround Kahar.

'Fucking Kahar—which sisterfucker is gonna save you now?'

Kahar feels the axe under the jute mat on which he's standing,
and sees with misty eyes Pakhot lifting his jackfruit onto his shoulder
and sliding across the mud to the cycle rickshaw in which sits
Firman. And who now puts his foot on Kahar's jackfruit which
Pakhot places before him. Firman had plenty of land, yet he couldn't
stop grabbing from the mouths of others.

'Raat bhar khaao piyo,
Din bhar araam karo.'

'Eat and drink all night,
Laze and rest all day.'

Suddenly Kahar pulled out the axe from under the mat, broke
through the circle and screamed, 'AWAWAWAWA!' the bloodcurd-
ling call of '46.

So many used to come rushing to that call, once upon a time.

But though the market is full of people, they are all lifeless dolls.
Only the song keeps playing on the loudspeaker. Kartik is too drunk
to notice the axe in Kahar's hand. He tries to kick Kahar, but falls
down flailing, the axe buried in his leg. Buried to the hilt. Kartik's leg
bleeds profusely. Those who'd been standing close to him now scatter
some distance away.

The others rush to fetch the fishmonger's large *boti* to cut up
Kahar. But Firman stops them. 'Beat him! Kick him! Kick him!
Harder!'

They fling Old Kahar to the ground and kick him, one after another, one hits him near his ear, his teeth break, his head starts to bleed. Blood and mud smear his body, cover his face. A kick to his ribs rolls him over to the side. Then another kick lands on his back, and he rolls over. Then rolls back again. Covers his face. They try to stand on his stomach, digging in their heels. They rip off his clothes, strip him naked. Nalish pisses on the mat in front of Kahar's fruit stand. Everyone else stands far away. Finally, Nalish and his gang leave, roaring and shouting. Firman's cycle rickshaw leads the way.

Old Kahar struggles back on his feet.

Yesterday, a Member of the Lok Sabha had come to meet him. He stares up at the sky and roars out his war cry all by himself, and then turns to looks at the people around him. The naked and blood-smeared Old Kahar says, 'Why did you go away? Come back, you bastards! Who can take away my fortune? No mother has birthed such a son who can. Which bastard will rob me? My fortune can't be taken from me, it can't. No one can. My fortune is the sky—can you take it away? Come here, you sons of bitches—my fortune is the land—you'll take it? I'll just dig my way into the heart of it. What will you take from me? How will you take it away? Come, you cowards, come! There's no one for me, no one! I'll go mad, I'll go mad again! Come! AWAWAWAWA!'

Kahar spits. Blood and saliva and bits of broken teeth spatter everywhere.

A little boy comes up and wraps a gamcchha around him. The battery-powered loudspeakers are still blaring out music. A police van arrives. Firman had informed them beforehand. The superintendent and his three armed constables, their heavy boots clomping along the mud, their guns swinging, the bayonets near their waists.

They arrest Old Kahar for assault and battery in a public place and take him away.

4 + 1

1.

It'd rained all day that day. Though not hard enough to flood the streets. A cold wind. Barely any daylight. Even though the tram driver hadn't been especially alert, he'd pulled the brakes at the right moment. And because it'd just rounded a corner, the tram hadn't been moving very fast either. But before the brakes could scratch and bite into the rails and the tram draw to a halt, the crash had already occurred. The two in front suffered minor injuries. The two at the back were unscathed. One had a cut on their forehead, the other had hurt their nose, their teeth and gums as well. Both were bleeding. (According to those who'd rushed to help.) Besides these four, there was a fifth—he was dead. Wrapped in black plastic, and tied to a wooden cot. Often, such funereal cots are decorated with flowers or incense sticks. There was none of that here. Later it was discovered that near the head of the corpse, wrapped in a dirty rag, were the following: a broken pair of dark glasses, a few stubs of chalksticks, some shreds of paper and half a thin-arrowroot biscuit. A faint hope had arisen that the pieces of paper might offer some clue. But they didn't. They bore nothing but a few meaningless scribbles. By some stretch of the imagination you could perhaps discover some meaning in them, but that would be meaningless too.

The one who'd been the most frightened was the tram driver. As
he should have been, because he'd seen them coming the moment
he'd rounded the corner. Coming at the tram with the corpse.
Heading straight at them. He'd stayed standing in his cage, completely stunned. There were hardly any people on the street. Yet a
small crowd gathered in no time. Then everyone got scared. Phone
call were made. The police arrived.

The four corpse bearers hadn't budged since they'd been hit by
the tram. They hadn't let the tram move either until the police arrived
and took them away. The two in front had blood streaming down
their faces. The crowd had told them to move aside. A few enthusi-
astic young men thought that that the men must be so high, their
pleas were falling on deaf ears. As it is, it was cloudy, it was raining, it
was hard to see. On top of that, even though the buildings in this
neighbourhood were old, they were rather tall, although the new
shops on their ground floors were all brightly lit. Every evening,
when the sun set, the shadows grew thick and dense. That day, the
shadows were even darker. Those intelligent citizens who could see
through what was behind what, they had said this must be a
gimmick, a *stunt*. That, the dead body was actually alive. And that the
corpse bearers were actors, all of them. That the whole thing was a
plot. Perhaps some perverse advertisement by a theatre group, or a
foolish prank by a bunch of bizarre clowns. The police, as in those
who'd come first, they had thought something like this too. Yet, this
lot didn't look like those loafers who dressed up corpses during Dol
for fun. Perhaps they're high on heroin or something. Ordinary
people and ordinary policemen think like this. Above them think
extraordinary people and extraordinary police. The newly employed
IPS officer had thought the same. It's not as if there'd been a huge

uproar. A few trams had halted one after the other. A crowd, a small knot of people. Four silent and speechless corpse bearers, and the dead body of a thin middle-aged man, wrapped in a black plastic sheet and tied up with rope. Near whose head, wrapped in a dirty rag, was one cracked black lens from a pair of glasses, one side of the black frame tied up with string, like the kind given away in free cataract-operation camps; the stubs of chalksticks so small that writing with them was impossible; a few torn pieces of paper marked with pluses, dots and a '5', or at least that's what was claimed after a series of investigations into what were no more than vague and random scribbles; and finally, a half-gnawed and now-soggy *thin-arrowroot* biscuit eaten by whom no one could tell. The dead man, at least, hadn't eaten it because the postmortem revealed no trace of biscuits. As soon as there was a line of halted trams, like flies, naked beggar boys, their bodies covered in sores, began to play at hopping on and off. Whatever it was, the young IPS officer calmly ordered the arrest of the four corpse bearers as well as the corpse. He even used the blue or green channel to arrange for the almost immediate transfer of the body to a morgue so that it could be preserved in ice to prevent deformation. Sand bags were placed around both the corpse and ice. The corpse could be a *booby trap*. The four corpse bearers were hand-cuffed and taken away for interrogation. The police report later revealed that their hands, when they were being handcuffed, did not have the same carefree air as when they had been clutching the legs of the body-bearing cot. And that all the while they had stood there staring straight ahead, their gazes unblinking. Even during their interrogations.

The IPS Officer hadn't been mistaken. The Bombay blast, the Calcutta blast, the blasts in South India and Pakistan-aided terrorism—in these fearful times, neither the Centre nor the states could afford any risks. He knew from reading Lenin that the Far Left and the Far Right were very good friends. These four famished, savage, scorch-skinned men, he needed to know what they were. Yes, 'Carlos' had been captured. But so what? Where was Tiger Memon? The mystery of the film actor who flew out of the window of a multi-storeyed building! The son of Nargis! RDX. AK-56. *Drugs*. Uranium and plutonium smuggling. Does India have nuclear power or doesn't it? Whether it did or it didn't, in such a situation, no discrepancy could be ignored. Nor has it been. After all, real life isn't *Roja* or *1942: A Love Story*.

2.

Before the interrogation, the examination of the corpse revealed that no organ in the thin old man's body had been exempt from insult. When an organ was injured or weakened by disease, a good doctor referred to it as an 'insult'. For example, if a person's liver has been afflicted by jaundice twice, then, if the doctor is a good one, they'll say that the liver has been 'insulted' twice. The dead body which lay on the cot, wrapped in black plastic and tied up with rope—that dead body's liver, kidneys, bladder, stomach, penis, eyes, scrotum, all had been 'insulted' multiple times. Recently, research in America had revealed that religion, poetry, love, envy, justice, thievery, hunger, sexuality, loves for one's wife, concern for one's children, the desire to rape, silence, taste in music, all of these were products of the head, or more accurately, of individual sections of the brain contained inside in the skull. The thin dead body's brains had not yet been dissected in the light of this research, though the good thing was that it was safely stored in an extremely cold morgue room. Paid for with government money. Therefore, the body was awaiting research.

The interrogation of the four corpse bearers had begun politely enough, to coax and cajole some words out of them. Those who are subjected to such skilful wordplay, they are bound to fall into trap after trap. But in this case it yielded no results. Because none of the four spoke a word. Everyone, meaning everyone who interrogates, wasn't always adept at this skilled form of interrogation. Rather, they resorted to beatings, to threats, to stopping at nothing until they got what they wanted. Some say it's all deliberate. And some say it happens in the heat of the moment. Either way, this interrogation began with the two whose faces hadn't been injured by the collision. That is, the two who'd been holding the two rear legs of the cot. Slapping them proved ineffective. As did kicking them while they hung upside down from the ceiling. Had the young IPS not intervened then, something truly deadly might have taken place. He put a stop to the second style of interrogation. A bit of medical treatment and those two sat up again in a few days. Then all four were sent off to the doctor.

3.

There's no point in getting into the details of simple procedures such as shining a light into the eyes, tapping the soles of the feet or the knees. All four had electrodes stuck to their heads. At this point we should make it clear to the reader that they should not at all mistake this to be the third form of interrogation. Science is not torture, although torture uses science. After examining several graphs on the *monitoring machine*, the specialist doctors held a council meeting. The *report* in English which they gave the head of police, and which the head of police kept a Xerox copy of before passing on the original to the Ministry of Home Affairs, and of which they kept a Xerox copy before passing the original on to someone at an even higher level, contained words and phrases such as 'No evoked potential in auditory/visual cortex on peripheral sensory stimulation' or 'sensory aphasia' or 'sensory-neural deficit', etc., and many other such whose simple meaning was that the four corpse bearers were blind, deaf and dumb. If someone is blind and deaf, they're bound to be dumb. And if someone is truly this way, then establishing communication with them is impossible. It had been impossible for them too. If you fed them, that is, if you gave them a plate full of food, they could eat. But one couldn't tell if they could smell the food or not. They never showed a change in expression. Never blinked. Didn't listen. Didn't see. Didn't speak. Wouldn't ever listen or see, either. And of speaking—there was no question of that at all. There was no way of knowing anything about them. They are imprisoned somewhere, and alongside, their original report, a Xerox *copy* duly saved, is heading up from one level to the next. It will reach the President one day, and then have to stop. But there will still be no way of finding out anything about these four deaf, dumb and blind corpse bearers.

4.

The dead body lies in an ultra-modern morgue. A few American billionaires had their own dead bodies preserved in even *more* ultra-modern morgues. In the hope that science, in the near future, would break through such horizons that they could be brought back to life. After a few hundred years, they would wake up again, and, skipping several generations, resume their businesses and enjoy the good life.

Such thoughts and desires were not meant to be entertained by the dead body we are speaking of here. Although, if he could ever be resurrected, then this mystery could have been solved. The young IPS officer, of course, was not thinking along these lines.

We've already mentioned that those four had been imprisoned. Behind thick iron bars. Under lock and key. Guards, day and night, in shifts. A small grille-covered square vent, high up in the wall. Through it, sometimes sunlight, sometimes the glow of the moon slopes into the room. When the sun sets, or the moon wanes, the light disappears, like an elusive cat. The four sit in silence. Sometimes a stray sparrow pecks at the grille from outside. Sometimes a small breath of wind enters and, at the sight of them, halts in its tracks. Their eyes never seem to blink. The four of them sit on the floor in silence. The sentries don't like standing guard there, especially at night. It was rumoured that they used to whisper then, even burst out laughing. That young IPS officer still visits occasionally, though we cannot call him young for very much longer for time is passing. Only in the room of the four corpse bearers does time seem to be standing still.

Whose dead body was it? What was his name? Did he have any family or friends? How did he die? Who are the four corpse bearers? Which crematorium were they going to that day? How would they have got there? How did such an incident actually take place?

If anyone has information pertaining to this matter, it is a public request to them to come forward to the appropriate authorities. The authorities are waiting.

No Head? So What?

Oh woe upon Birinchi's oily shiny-slick mishhapen head! Every cell of its grey matter filled with trickery, opportunism and profiteering, oh woe, woe! Didn't you once make a killing on the *baby-food* black market, and then weren't you caught red-handed and paraded around the neighbourhood in disgrace, my dear? Where's that ghostly skull now, my man? If a pigeon or a griffin or some other such bastardly bird, in the dark of the night sky, like a lovelorn creature from some ancient age, sorrowfully shrieks 'Birinchi, where are you!', then Birinchi's head will not stick out from the shit-canal and say 'Here I am.' That song that made him sad, 'You're mine, I'm yours, guess who I am to you,' Birinchi will never listen to that song again.

By the unwavering laws of the whoremarket, Birinchi has been offed by either 007 or the author. He's a good man, just has a few flaws. The setting: Darjipara Park. Every other neighbourhood is dealing with a bout of breakdance. The sound of cracking skulls. The moon is out and burning bright enough to burn witches.

Birinchi had broken out in a sweat. That afternoon, he'd stuffed himself with ilish-fish oil, fried eggs, kochu-leaf-and-fish-head curry, hot and spicy. The ilish have a lot of *heat*. From the oil. He didn't go back to his shop, slept with his nose buried in his pillow. When he woke up, his head felt stuffed and steaming, hot and heavy. He sat there for a while, silent and stolid. Cloud, cloud, cloudy, who's behind the veil? The maid brings him tea. He drinks it. He lights a cigarette, his head clears. He must go today. His body is yearning to go.

This 'going' happens in more ways than it is possible to enumerate. Perhaps Gour Pal tells Nobinchand, 'I've been coming and going for such a long time. It's not bad, not at all. But today I want to eat from your hands, brother.' Nobinchand goes to Madhobi. Gour Pal goes too.

A bunch of skinny old men sit at the oil company's *surplus* pool. If you say 'The one who ploughs, owns the land', they retort: 'Now you'll say "He who owns the palanquin, owns the bride".' They get paid each month, but do no work. Every day when they meet, they say, 'I swear, never again, enough is enough.' Another old man says, 'All because of you. As soon as it's evening, your grumbling'll begin.' And that is indeed what happens. As soon as it's almost evening, one of the old men says, 'What! Shall we go for a bit? Such a long tradition, is it right to let it go just like that?'

'No, brother. I've got a home and family.'

'I swear, this is the last time. If you're running short, then say so. You can pay later'

In the end, they end up going. A variety of people go for a variety of needs, a variety of reasons. This is how people end up in whorehouses. All those who go every day, if they all agreed to march in procession, one would be absolutely gobsmacked. A few go alone, go in groups, peep like toms and slip inside, dillydally for a bit at the paan and cigarette shops but in the end they end up going. First by minibus, then by double-decker, a bottle tucked underneath his arm, Birinchi finally arrived at the red-light district. Then the saw-toothed moon was swimming through the hairy chest of the sky, and the fumes from the diesel and petrol and food had formed an oily and entirely different kind of canopy beneath the clouds.

That story, that one about the memsaheb hostel . . . In this context, one should mention that Birinchi had benefited from the fruits of the scientific and technological revolutions. Later we may come to know how creatively some prostitutes had utilized these same developments. Weren't newspapers covered with ads for ribbed *condoms*? And over there, at the monthly gatherings, organized by the members of his neighbourhood market's businessmen's association, they first played XX and later XXX *blue films* on a rented video player; Birinchi watched them regularly and was filled with joy. This year, Birinchi's older son had bought a Hero Honda, so he'd become a bit of a miser. When his wife Malotimala kept asking for a VCP, he said: 'A couple of rupees I've managed to save, and you won't let me. What a bother! Why this itch at this ripe old age?' His younger son is Chandu, he wants to buy a VCR, to make midnight films. He's *got* to buy him one. But it was like buying a defective cow; its udder would hang huge yet yield no milk. He couldn't watch XXX *blue films* at home, after all.

His mouth full of Pan Bahar, Birinchi lifts a leg to step up on the footpath but recoils at the pool of vomit lying there. Which fucker's thrown up here! Oof, what a sour smell! He shoves some more Pan Bahar into his mouth and slips into a lane. Madan comes forward. Familiar clients, unfamiliar clients, Madan always comes forward. His vest has 'Maradona' printed on it.

'What's up, Rental Madan! What do the elephants say?'

'Sir, call me Rental Madan, Mental Madan, whatever you want, whatever your heart desires. There aren't no elephants for you today.'

'What do you mean!'

'The crowd's real heavy today. Room after room, clients in every one of them. Do you know what the *case* is? I'm totally stumped myself. Yesterday and the day before, I was swatting flies. Today it's fucking *house full*. It's turning into a *canter* is what it is.'

'Alta, Phulrani, your Chunmun, even the Telengi whore, the one who had jaundice?'

'What am I telling you? All the way from Tikiapara, Bongaon, from wheresthat Gore, from Boral—they've come in hordes today. If they came by taxi, then even the driver locked the car and went inside. There's even a group of sahebs from the ships. What sales, how sweet they smell!'

'So this body that's come all the way, it won't be put to any use? You'll just send it back? Get me in somehow, my son. I'm even willing to pay a little more.'

'Did I ever talk about more or less? Of course, there is *one* place. Will you go?'

'And that place is empty despite this crowd? She's not that noseless-earless thing, is she, the one who perches on top of the lamp post in Bhallukpara?'

'No, no, don't be silly. This is *guaranteed* stuff. You can negotiate the price when you meet. Only one flaw, though—'

'Why don't you speak clearly?'

'Sir, see, front and back, it's all there. Only the head's missing.'

'What? No head? She's . . . alive, right? No, no, never mind, I don't want to get trapped in a *murder case*.'

'You're really something else, sir. What nonsense you talk. There's nothing else available, all the rooms are full. Despite that, I hunt out a *satis* piece for you. And you're just finding fault after fault.'

'*Satis* piece? You're the one who said she has no head!'

'So what if she has no head! Head, heads—do you have any business with her head? Will you fuck her head or what!'

Birinchi grows more and more agitated. Huffs and puffs and tries to arrive at a compromise. Beside his dark and stubby nose, beads of oil prick through his skin.

'All right, then. Let's go.'

Birinchi hurries after Madan, tripping every now and then, until they arrive.

An ancient narrow staircase, the bricks exposed. If you tried to carry a corpse down it, the strain of it might kill you too. The arch swoops so low, one suddenly finds it hitting one's forehead. The air vents up in the ceiling reek of bats. This is just the *video*. The *audio* track plays odd bits of songs, some laughter and the radio. A balcony running all the way around, and a courtyard in the middle where someone is noisily washing clothes. The smell of country and foreign liquor.

Madan knocks on the door three times. Inside, the whine of an old, heavy, DC-area fan. A red light. Now, a small tube light comes on with a flutter. Birinchi tightens his arm around the booze bottle. Madan pushes the doors open. The doors in turn push aside an old sari curtain.

'Go, go through the curtain, go in.'

The headless whore is sitting beside the bed. As soon as Birinchi enters, she stands up. She's wearing a blue nylon sari. No blouse. Dark, but quite voluptuous. All the way up to her neck, and then suddenly empty. No head.

Birinchi hears Madan whistling as he makes his way back.

The headless whore is speechless, but not helpless. A couple of tin boxes covered by a saree, and on top a vase filled with fresh plastic flowers. Beside that, a cassette recorder. The whore first presses a switch and turns off the tube light. Now in the room there's just a dim red glow. Then she turns on the cassette recorder. It's a while until the magnetic tape turns and begins to play. A crackling sound. And then her voice comes on: just one *dialogue*, repeated over and over: 'You want to sit, or hear a song? You want to sit, or hear a song? You want to sit, or hear a song?'

Birinchi is more amused than afraid. He's got an *idea* too. He'll also play a cassette at his shop: 'Cash today, pay tomorrow. Cash today, pay tomorrow. Cash today, pay tomorrow . . .'

Birinchi places the booze bottle on a white, crocheted tablecloth-covered table. Lights a cigarette and bursts out laughing. The whore presses the Stop button. Then Fast Forward. Then Play. This time, peals of metallic laughter. Probably recorded a long time ago, perhaps during the Kali Puja bhashan, because in-between the bouts of laughter, you could hear shouts of 'Glory to Mother Kali!' and the beating of drums.

The laughter plays on, the laughter in the red light. The whore touches Birinchi once, and then circles him. Blue nylon saree in the red light—oh! A delectable delicacy indeed! She sashays across the room, shuts the door. Brings two glasses on the table, patterned with flowers and deer, puts them on the table. Takes out the cassette, puts a new one in. Tarzan. The heroine is singing out to all kinds of wild animals, calling them close: Mere paas aao naa, mere saath gaao naa. Why don't you come close to me, why don't you sing a song with me. The animals grunt in response.

Birinchi knocks back drink after drink. Grunts. Flexes his muscles like a wrestler. Gets ready. Even though he's high, he's still got his wits about him. He thinks: the head must've been cut off with something really sharp. Like a guillotine, maybe even a paper-cutting *machine*. Or maybe her head had never grown at all. So many things were known to happen. Even though he gave it so much thought, he ended up making a fool of himself. Trying to kiss her, he found himself straining into empty air. Force of habit. He won't kiss her again, won't search for a mouth.

At the mouth of the lane was parked a taxi, its lights turned off. Three infamous gangsters sat inside—Bongshi, Chhobelaal and Kelepawcha. The real taxi driver was lying in Taratala, by the side of the road, unconscious, his mouth stuffed with a gamchha and his head bleeding profusely. These antisocial elements are evil indeed. They've become so overconfident that they have no sense of what to do where. Last year, on 16 August, that is, when the Independence Day flowers hadn't yet had time to wilt, it was a Sunday, the DC (South) went himself to no less than Alimuddin Street and arrested the Magnificent Seven gangsters who were then warring. The 'Soldier' gang and the 'Steelbody' gang were locked in battle so deadly that Sheikh Tallu alias Guli died when a bomb burst in his hand. The newspapers reported: 'At one point, the police had to lathicharge the rowdy public . . . On Sunday night, a raid on Alimuddin Street resulted in the discovery of a few freshly made bombs. Recently, another police raid in the same place had yielded a vast quantity of illegal drugs . . . ' (*Anandabazaar Patrika*, 18 August). If this is what happens in Alimuddin Street, then one can easily imagine what can happen in other small-fry neighbourhoods and necks of the woods. Already there were the unnatural deaths of housewives. *Suicide notes.*

Arrested husbands. On top of that *tablets, heroin, smack, brown sugar*—tell me Birinchi, which mother's bonny-faced son will row you across this river, eh?

Lo and behold, O dark night! The body of the moon grows weary. Early that night, she'd blazed with enough light to burn witches. Now she's the yellowish glow of a dying funeral pyre. The legs of the city had slipped off the pyre's edge—a slight nudge from the dom's bamboo pole and it rolls back into the flames. Sparks from the charcoal spit and splutter into the air. The smell of burning flesh, burning hair, walk from door to door, knocking. A pitch-black cat jumps onto the street, runs across to the other side. Its eyes glow like the Big Dog in the sky.

Birinchi lurches his way out onto the street. Though the taxi is far away, Kelepawcha's expert vision, like a *laser* beam, penetrates its scratched-over window glass and swiftly searches out Birinchi's presence, and spies, sparkling in the light of the street lamp, a fine gold chain nestled among the folds of fat at his neck. Birinchi was singing : 'When the Other Side comes calling, Know who I am to you.'

The taxi door swings open with a crack, like the sound of a neck snapping in two.

'Need a taxi, babu? Want to go home?'

Birinchi laughs and says 'No head? So what? The fun was just the same, my brother.'

Kelepawcha grabs him, bundles him into the taxi. Chhobelaal squeezes in beside them. The *meter* is turned *down*. Bongshi *starts* the engine: Diesel Mark IV. The engine rattles way too much. The car shakes. Bongshi's a good driver. Changes gears as soon as the wheels begins to roll. Dodges the potholes, even though it's a stolen car. He doesn't think about it; he's just a good driver, that's all. He *slows* down near the main crossing. Glances left and right for police vans or Jeeps, then swerves left, parallel to the tram line.

Birinchi is vomiting nonstop. Chhobelaal holds his head close to the floor, but every time Birinchi retches, he bounces up again.

'He's puking, boss.'

'Turn him over, or he'll spray it everywhere.'

Birinchi pushes himself up, vomit foam and vomit strings hanging from his mouth. Midnight citylights glow outside. Bump into each other. One light sends many lights shooting here and there. Birinchi suddenly wants to burst out laughing. 'No head? So what! Oh, it was so good today! Hope you're driving in the right direction, brother?'

'You're in our care, you just sit tight. We'll make sure we take you home.'

'That's good. Home, and then straight to bed.'

Birinchi shuts his eyes but is overcome by alternating waves of song and vomit.

'You're mine, and I'm yours . . . aaarghhhhhhhh!'

Chhobelaal gets pissed off.

'This fucker's getting it all over my pants-shants, by god. Aye fatso . . . fatso!'

Birinchi looks up. And then embraces him. 'There! You have a head, I see!'

'What the fuck's he saying, boss? Says I've got a head?'

'Oof, you know nothing, brother. Truth is: No head? So what! I didn't miss it for a second.'

They stop the taxi beside the shit-canal. Far off in the distance, a few lights glimmer. Somewhere, an owl hoots. The stink of mud, shit, rotting weeds. An upturned rickshaw, its handle broken.

They rip the chain off Birinchi's neck. They tear his shirt to bits. Take his wristwatch. Take the sweaty wad of cash rolled into a ball and tucked into his vest. Throw away his pocket comb and filch his loose change. Then Bongshi holds down Birinchi's neck on the upturned rickshaw's footrest. Chhobelaal had never seen a decapitation before. He goes off to the canal, washes the vomit off his pants. Kelepawcha uses a dagger that's blunt on one side but butter-smooth-sharp on the other to slowly slice away at Birinchi's neck. The body's drunk, so it flutters less. Birinchi's body stays on the canal bank. His head they throw into the water. It drops into a clump of weeds which slowly begins to sink under its weight. The head falls upside down. The water soaks the hair, then the forehead, the eyes, the nose and then the lips. Fills the mouth. The bloody severed neck looks like a black hole in the moonlight, but then that too slips below the surface.

The taxi *starts* up. Reverses. Then speeds up the slope in first gear and roars its way up the canalside road. Falls into a pothole, grazes the *culvert* as it turns right and vanishes. The noise fades away. This time, the ring of the meter being down can't be heard.

It is rumoured that this game of decapitation was witnessed by none other than Uttam Kumar one early morning at the Maidan. And wasn't a skull-less skeleton unearthed at the Manohar Das Tarag during the Metro Rail construction? It's that old rule of history: the first time as tragedy, the second time as farce. Best to forget all that. We are now in *nineteen eighty-seven*.

The canal banks overflow with so many kinds of plants, rats, wild creepers, snail shells, filthy scum, rotten muck, decomposing-dog-and-dead-body juices. In its waters is submerged Birinchi's head. Nonchalant. The eyes slightly open, but underwater they look tightly shut. On the water's surface, eight-legged insects leap and bound their way across. Light from the nearest constellation, from several light years away, suddenly grows alert at the smell of blood close to the water before it crashes to the earth. Birinchi, did you know what beauty treatments are only possible in this dirty, filthy water? You're growing so handsome, boss!'

Birinchi, you keep going. We're with you. Long live Birinchi! May Birinchi be immortal! This fight is the fight for life, we have to win it, Birinchi! *What Birinchi thinks today, India thinks tomorrow. Three cheers for Birinchi. Hip hip hooray.* Birinchi, awake! Birinchi, arise and roar. O our Great and Holy Birinchi, the work you've begun is still undone. No head? So what? Birinchi *darling, sweet bastard.* Tumhara kya hua, Birinchi? What happened to you? Birinchi, do you speak French? *Vous parle français?* Birinchi, *good night.* Ay, you son of a bitch, Birinchi! *Don't be naughty,* Birinchi. Look, look at who's come to take you. Birinchi. Birinchi, *be A-Smart.* Birinchi, be *smart.* Shame, Birinchi, don't wipe away the shindoor. Don't break your shankha. Bi . . . Rin . . . Chi! Biri! Insat-1 Bi-Rinchi! Beep-beep Birinchi! Hey, brave Birinchi, awake, arise, *great* conman Birinchi-baba, rise you fucker—O Brave Birinchi, O Lionheart Birinchi, O Flapping-Farewell Birinchi, O Renunciate Birinchi, enough. Wake up now, dear father.

Birinchi is unperturbed. That is best. No head. He won't be needing the comb any more. Save the *saloon* money too. No thoughts. No worries. When Birinchi's mother was pregnant with him, her mother-in-law had said that since the milk for the payesh had curdled, it was bound to be a boy. Birinchi was born. Today, Birinchi is dead. No matter what, headless Birinchi and the headless whore do not have the same market value. Birinchi's historical role might have been put to an end, but that doesn't affect the rates of the headless whore.

How could the headless whore know via *remote control* that Birinchi was gone? Her comic sense was incredibly sharp. The moment her cassette recorder plays, her metallic laughter rings out through the city. Goes round and round. No head? So what? Is there any lack of amusement? Of comfort? A cassette-cassette laugh. A storm of laughter. No head? So what?

Today, the headless whore is very happy indeed.

TRANSLATOR'S NOTES

Nabarun Bhattacharya's stories contain several English words in Bengali transliteration; all such words have been italicized in the present volume.

PAGE 1 | 'Hero Honda': Joint venture between Hero Cycles of India and Honda Auto of Japan in 1983. Hero Honda two-wheelers quickly gained the largest market share in India.

PAGE 2 | 'Hawa hawa': Urdu, literally, 'Wind o wind'. A 1987 song by Pakistani singer Hasan Jahangir. Immensely popular in India, spawning many unapproved Bollywood adaptations.

PAGE 2 | 'Ek do teen, chaar paanch chhai': Hindi, literally, 'One two three, four five six'. Lyrics of a popular song from the 1988 Hindi film *Tezaab*.

PAGE 3 | 'Digha': Beach town on the coast of West Bengal. Popular travel destination among Bengalis.

PAGE 4 | 'Naxal': Left-wing extremist. Name derived from Naxalbari in Siliguri, West Bengal, site of an armed peasant revolt in 1967. The movement spread across Bengal and became inseparable from student movements, leading to harsh and often extrajudicial and lethal repression from the Indian National Congress–led government of West Bengal, especially between 1972 and 1977.

PAGE 5 | 'Ghapaghap': Onomatopoeia. Used to describe a rapid, violent action.

PAGE 6 | 'Folidol': Insecticide. Popular among farmers for its cost-effectiveness; notorious among everyone else for its widespread use in suicide.

PAGE 7 | 'kapaliks': Members of a tantric suborder of Shaivites (worshippers of the Hindu deity Shiva), associated with the motif of the skull (*kapala*) and transgressive sexual rituals.

PAGE 8 | 'Mor bhabonare ki haway matalo': Literally, 'What wind enthralls my mind!' Popular song by Rabindranath Tagore.

PAGE 9 | 'Nehru Bal Museum': Museum in Kolkata established to educate children through visual aids.

PAGE 10 | 'Baranagar Killing': Infamous massacre of around a hundred youths belonging to 'resistance groups' (Naxals) on 12–13 August 1971 in Baranagar, North Calcutta.

PAGE 17 | 'movie-ticket *blackers*': 'Blackers' used to buy up all tickets for a movie show to sell them at higher prices to the public.

PAGE 21 | 'peto-bomb': Homemade explosive device characterized by its round shape (hence 'peto', that is, potbellied in Bangla) and outer shell made of jute. Widely used by Naxalites and still occasionally used in the absence of more advanced explosives.

PAGE 21 | 'Hare Krishna Hare Ram': Reference to the lyrics of a song from the 1971 Hindi film *Hare Rama Hare Krishna*, starring Dev Anand and Zeenat Aman, among others.

PAGE 21 | '*Ankh Micholi*': 1972 Hindi film starring Bharathi and Rakesh Roshan.

PAGE 22 | 'Kishore Kumar': Popular Indian singer and actor, working in many languages including Bengali and Hindi, active through the 1950s to '80s.

PAGE 22 | 'Jungle mein mangal manayenge hum': Censorship imposed by the Central Board of Film Censors (later, Certification) in India prevented the direct reference to sex or its portrayal. This was substituted by visual (lovers biting into the same apple, two flowers touching each other) and lyrical innuendo.

PAGE 27 | 'dom': A formerly 'untouchable' caste in Hindu society whose members are primarily engaged in creamting dead bodies.

PAGE 28 | 'take Durga to the river': The last night of the ten-day Bengali festival of Durga Puja in autumn is marked by the casting of the idol of Goddess Durga into the River Ganga. The procession accompanying the idol on its last journey is usually marked by loud music, applause, dancing and lighting of fire crackers.

PAGE 34 | 'Corporation': Kolkata Municipal Corporation, the civic body responsible, among others, for the city's cleanliness.

PAGE 43 | 'kulaks': Russian term used by Soviet Communists to deride landowning farmers of the last days of the Russian empire.

PAGE 43 | Monument: Shaheed Minar, formerly known as Ochterlony Monument, and still widely referred to as simply the 'Monument'—a 48-metre tall memorial column in the Esplanade area of Central Calcutta, a popular landmark in the city.

PAGE 47 | 'shindoor': Vermillion that is traditionally applied by married Hindu women to their hair parting as one of the symbols of their married status.

PAGE 49 | 'Duokko, khuniyalko, ladenakko': Various parts of India have kite fights: flying kites on manja (string infused with glass dust) with the objective of severing the opponent's string. This is specialized language of these kite fights.

PAGE 69 | 'satis': Slang term, short for 'satisfaction'. In this context, 'sexy'.

PAGE 69 | 'Parde mein rehne do': A song from the Hindi film Shikar (1968) sung by Asha Bhosle; not a conventional qawwali, which is a form of Sufi Islamic devotional singing.

PAGE 69 | 'loadshedding': Local term for a power cut. Technical definition is an intentional electrical shutdown to prevent more widespread grid failure.

PAGE 71 | 'Hari Bol': Bengali, literally, 'Say, "Hari"!' Chant invoking a name of Lord Krishna.

PAGE 76 | 'Teli': Hindu caste traditionally involved in the pressing of oil.

PAGE 76 | 'Meghalaya jackpot': Until 2007, 13 Indian states, including Meghalaya in North-East India, organized state lotteries for supplementary revenue.

PAGE 77 | 'Tarun Bose': Legendary Bengali footballer of the 1970s who played for East Bengal Club; was instrumental in the 5–0 victory over the other major Bengali football team, Mohun Bagan, in the 1975 IFA Shield finals.

PAGE 86 | 'flapperoo': Bangla: 'Fyataru'. Onomatopoeic word made up by Bhattacharya to designate his magic-realist set of characters who can fly; they recur occasionally throughout his oeuvre.

PAGE 96 | 'Tata': Tata Group of Industries, one of the largest and oldest multinational business conglomerates from India, established in 1868.

PAGE 96 | 'Sri Aurobindo': Aurobindo Ghose (1872–1950), Indian nationalist leader up to 1910; thereafter, a Hindu spiritualist.

PAGE 96 | 'the Mother': Mira Alfassa (1878–1973), spiritual collaborator of Sri Aurobindo, known to her followers as 'the Mother'. Instrumental in the founding of the Sri Aurobindo Ashram in Pondicherry in South India in the 1920s as well as the nearby experimental township of Auroville in 1968.

PAGE 97 | 'Complan': A health drink aimed at children and adolescents, sold in the form of a flavoured powder; became especially popular in India in the 1980s.

PAGE 102 | 'Tebhaga': Significant peasant movement in Bengal in 1946–47, led by the Communist Party of India, with the demand to reduce the harvest share of landlords from half to one-third ('te': three, 'bhaga': division).

PAGE 102 | 'botis': Bladed instruments used to cut meat and vegetables.

PAGE 104 | 'Charu Majumdar': (1919–1972) leader of the Naxalite movement in Bengal until his death in the custody of Kolkata Police. Espoused Mao Zedong's violent revolutionary methods, advocating that Indian peasants and lower-class indigenous people forcibly overthrow the government of 'the upper classes'.

PAGE 104 | 'Khanpur': Village in South Dinajpur district, West Bengal. Population primarily consisted of Santhal indigenous people, who were involved in the Tebhaga Movement. On 20 February 1947, 22 people were killed here in police firing.

PAGE 105 | 'Cow-and-Calf': Between 1971 and 1977, the electoral symbol of the Indian National Congress (R) founded and led by then prime minister Indira Gandhi.

PAGE 111 | 'martyr family': Those involved in the Indian Struggle for Independence (popularly called 'freedom fighters') and their dependent relatives have been regularly given a monthly pension from the Government of India. A monthly allowance is also given to the families of Indian soldiers killed in action.

PAGE 116 | 'Dol': Dol Jatra, Hindu Bengali festival of colours similar to Holi in form, dedicated to Lord Krishna and consort Radha.

PAGE 117 | 'blue or green channel': Priority 'channels' assigned to specific routes on streets for emergency transportation such as for organ delivery.

PAGE 118 | 'Roja': 1992 Tamil/Hindi film directed by Mani Ratnam set against the backdrop of Kashmiri separatism.

PAGE 118 | '1942: A Love Story': 1994 Hindi film directed by Vidhu Vinod Chopra set against the backdrop of the Indian Struggle for Independence in 1942.

PAGE 124 | 'Pan Bahar': Popular brand of mouth freshener; also an ingredient for the preparation of 'pan' or folded betel leaf; contains tobacco and areca nut that stain the mouth red.

PAGE 127 | 'Mere paas aao naa, mere saath gaao naa': Song from Hindi film Adventures of Tarzan (1985), misquoted in the Bangla. Original lyric: 'Mere paas aaoge, mere saath naachoge?' Trans.: 'Come close, why don't you? Dance with me, why don't you?' The musical sequence has a scene in which Tarzan plucks a banana and tenderly feeds it to his love interest.

PAGE 128 | 'Alimuddin Street': Kolkata street on which the headquarters of the Communist Party of India (Marxist), or CPI(M), are located. At the time the story was written, 1987, CPI(M) was the principal political party in the long-running Left Front government of West Bengal. It could be said that the state was practically governed from Alimuddin Street and that it was the primary seat of power.

PAGE 131 | 'Uttam Kumar': (1926–1980) Legendary Bengali film star.

PAGE 131 | 'Manohar Das Tarag': Water tank, originally built in 1857, in the Maidan area of Kolkata.